LOST IN LAS VEGAS

OTHER BOOKS BY MELODY CARLSON:

Carter House Girls series

Mixed Bags (Book One)
Stealing Bradford (Book Two)
Homecoming Queen (Book Three)
Viva Vermont! (Book Four)

Girls of 622 Harbor View series

Project: Girl Power (Book One)
Project: Mystery Bus (Book Two)
Project: Rescuing Chelsea (Book Three)
Project: Take Charge (Book Four)
Project: Raising Faith (Book Five)
Project: Run Away (Book Six)
Project: Ski Trip (Book Seven)
Project: Secret Admirer (Book Eight)

Books for Teens

The Secret Life of Samantha McGregor series
Diary of a Teenage Girl series
TrueColors series
Notes from a Spinning Planet series
Degrees series
Piercing Proverbs
By Design series

Women's Fiction

These Boots Weren't Made for Walking
On This Day
An Irish Christmas
The Christmas Bus
Crystal Lies
Finding Alice
Three Days

Grace Chapel Inn Series, including

Hidden History
Ready to Wed
Back Home Again

carter house girls

LOST IN LAS VEGAS

melody carlson

ZONDERVAN®

ZONDERVAN.com/
AUTHORTRACKER
follow your favorite authors

We want to hear from you. Please send your comments about this book to us in care of zreview@zondervan.com. Thank you.

ZONDERVAN®

Lost in Las Vegas
Copyright © 2009 by Melody Carlson

Requests for information should be addressed to:

Zondervan, Grand Rapids, Michigan 49530

Library of Congress Cataloging-in-Publication Data: Applied for
ISBN 978-0-310-71492-7

Interior design by Christine Orejuela-Winkelman

Printed in the United States of America

09 10 11 12 13 14 15 16 • 22 21 20 19 18 17 16 15 14 13 12 11 10 9 8 7 6 5 4 3 2 1

LOST IN LAS VEGAS

"REMIND ME TO NEVER, ever star in another high school musical again." Eliza sighed dramatically as she poured her coffee. It was the Sunday morning after the final performance of *South Pacific*, and DJ suspected that Eliza was just fishing for compliments. Not that she hadn't already gotten plenty. And last night, she'd been presented with a huge bouquet of roses. DJ knew they were from Eliza's parents, but Eliza received them as if they had been an Oscar.

"But what if Mr. Harper does *High School Musical* in the spring?" asked Kriti with wide dark eyes. DJ could tell by the way Kriti said this she was hoping he would. Eliza probably was too.

"That is so last week," said Taylor.

"Meaning you wouldn't participate in it?" Eliza pushed a long strand of blonde hair over her shoulder and sat up straighter, looking directly at Taylor like this was a personal challenge.

Taylor rolled her eyes and then reached for the fruit platter. "Meaning, I don't really want to think about it right now.

Sheesh, Eliza, didn't you just ask us to remind you *never* to be in another musical?"

"Eliza is probably just trying to secure her next starring role," said Rhiannon. Then she frowned like she hadn't really meant it to sound like that. "And why shouldn't she?" she added quickly. "Eliza was absolutely fantastic as Nurse Nellie. Everyone said so."

"And it's obvious that Eliza will never let us forget she was a star," teased Casey.

"*Was.*" Taylor chuckled. "As in she's a has-been now."

Some of the girls snickered, but Eliza just glared at Taylor.

Then as if she'd just started listening, Grandmother cleared her throat, closed the open date book that she'd been studying, and looked at the girls. "I see there are only two weeks remaining until winter break, ladies." She shook her head sadly. "I just can't believe that it's already December. It seems like only yesterday that you girls arrived at Carter House. My, my, how time flies."

"And the Winter Ball is next Saturday," Eliza reminded them. As if anyone could've forgotten with posters plastered all over the school. DJ was still unsure whether she should go. Conner had asked her, but she hadn't agreed. Even though Haley hadn't returned to school yet, it still made DJ uncomfortable to be seen as more than "just friends" with Conner. And DJ knew that Haley's swim-team buddies were probably reporting to her.

"My mother and I are shopping for gowns today," continued Eliza. She glanced at her roommate. "And Kriti too, of course."

"I already have my dress," said Taylor. "A little something my mother sent over from Milan while she was performing there last month."

DJ could tell this little dig was aimed directly at Eliza. The two girls had been going at it steadily for the last couple of weeks. It first started when Eliza's boyfriend, Harry, gave Taylor a "shoulder massage" while backstage during a rehearsal for the musical. DJ had observed the two of them and had no doubt that Harry was flirting. But what Harry didn't know was that Eliza had been watching too. Of course, Harry denied everything, and then Eliza blamed Taylor for the incident. Yet, in a way, DJ was glad Eliza and Taylor were at odds again. They had all experienced those two power forces united during last month's ski trip—and it had been a rather frightening experience. Sort of like it might be if Russia and China ever got together.

"My mother offered to shop for a gown in Paris for me," said Eliza—her attempt at one-upping Taylor. "But I told her to wait. I wouldn't want to risk having a dress that fit poorly."

"That's why God invented alterations, Eliza," said Taylor. "Or perhaps you don't have such conveniences down south."

"I don't see why girls think they need to go out and spend a bunch of money on something new for a stupid dance," said Casey. She glanced at Rhiannon, and DJ suspected that Casey was trying to make her feel better. "I mean, you'll wear that dress like one time. What a waste!"

"So what do you intend to wear?" asked Eliza with a bored sort of interest. "Your Doc Martins and something with spikes?"

Casey made a face. "Actually, I might go eighties retro. Like Madonna or Blondie."

"Right." Eliza turned up her nose. "The Winter Ball theme is White Christmas, and we're supposed to dress in a fifties style of Hollywood elegance."

"You take those posters literally?" asked Casey.

"They suggested dresses in Christmas colors of red, green, or white." Eliza continued like she was reading it from a brochure.

"I think it'll be pretty," said Kriti.

"I intend to look for something sparkly in white to show off my tan," said Eliza.

"Fake tan." Taylor pushed a curly dark strand of hair away from her face and laughed. "My dress is black."

"It figures." Eliza snickered.

"I'm going to wear green," said Rhiannon quickly, like she was trying to keep this from escalating.

"What do you mean 'it figures'?" demanded Taylor.

"Everyone else will look Christmassy in red, green, or white, and the vamp will show up wearing black." Eliza laughed.

"Speaking of winter break," said Grandmother loudly. "What exactly are your plans, ladies?" She opened her date book and picked up her silver pen. "I'd like to make note of it now, if you don't mind."

"I'll be in France for Christmas," Eliza announced proudly.

"So you'll be flying directly to France from Connecticut?" inquired Grandmother.

"Actually, I'll spend the first week or so in Kentucky," admitted Eliza. "Visiting with friends and family. Then my older siblings and I will travel together just before Christmas. My mother said the rooms aren't completely renovated yet. Her designer, a well-known Parisian, promises to have it completed before Christmas Eve."

"La – TI – da," said Casey.

Grandmother frowned at Casey. "So, how about you, Miss Atwood? When will you be departing for California?"

"The same day that school is out."

Grandmother made note of this.

"And I'll be leaving the day after school is out," said Rhiannon.

Grandmother's brows lifted with curiosity. "To go where, dear?"

"To an aunt who lives in Maine."

Grandmother smiled. "That's nice. I didn't know you had an aunt, Rhiannon."

"I didn't either. She's actually a great-aunt and . . ." Rhiannon paused as if unsure. "My mother may be joining me up there."

"Really?" Grandmother looked a bit skeptical, and everyone else got quiet. They all knew that Rhiannon's mother was in drug rehab—the lockdown kind.

"Yes. If my aunt signs something, they'll release her for the holidays."

"Very interesting." Grandmother looked at Kriti now. "I assume you'll be in New York?"

Kriti nodded happily. "Yes. We have some relatives coming from India to visit. My mother is very excited."

"Well, I'm sure you'll have a delightful Christmas." Grandmother frowned with realization. "I suppose you don't call it Christmas, do you, Kriti?"

Kriti looked slightly embarrassed. "It's a different sort of holiday, Mrs. Carter. We celebrate things like love, affection, sharing, and the renewing of family bonds."

"That sounds lovely." Grandmother looked at Taylor now. "And what will you be doing during the holidays, dear?"

Taylor sighed. "My mother has invited me to tour with her."

Grandmother's eyes lit up. She was a huge fan of Eva Perez. "Where will she be touring? Europe still?"

"I wish. No, she'll be in the Southwest by then. And it looks like we'll be spending Christmas in Las Vegas."

Eliza snickered. "Charming."

Taylor tossed her a warning glance. "Hey, Las Vegas has its perks."

"Most important is that you're with family, Taylor." Grandmother smiled. "Isn't that what Christmas is all about?"

Taylor shrugged. "I guess."

Grandmother looked at DJ. "Now, you're still certain you don't want to join your father and his family for Christmas, Desiree?"

"No, Grandmother." DJ tried not to show frustration. But she and Grandmother had already been over this. The last place DJ wanted to be during Christmas break was with her father's happy little stepfamily. It was bad enough that this would be her first Christmas without her mother. But to be stuck playing the live-in babysitter to the toddler twins was unimaginable.

"Well, I'm sure that we'll have a delightful time right here at home." Grandmother smiled at DJ. "Perhaps we'll have the general over."

DJ got sympathetic glances from Rhiannon and Casey and maybe even Kriti. Not that she wanted their pity. Eliza just smiled smugly. And Taylor, well, she was a hard one to read.

But later that day after DJ and Rhiannon got back from church, Taylor asked DJ if she was happy about her "holiday plans."

DJ groaned as she flopped onto her bed. "Holiday plans? Like I planned any of this?"

Taylor laughed. "Yeah, I guess not."

"I'll be fine," DJ assured her. "I'll catch up on sleep and reading."

"Maybe Conner will be around to keep you entertained," Taylor said in a sexy-sounding, teasing tone.

"Conner is going with his family to Montana for two weeks."

"Bummer."

"Tell me about it."

"I know!" Taylor exclaimed. "You'll come out to Las Vegas and visit me for Christmas."

DJ just laughed. "Oh, yeah, like that's going to happen."

"Why not?" Taylor looked slightly hurt.

"Seriously, Christmas in Las Vegas?"

"Why not?"

"Well, besides the fact that it sounds totally crazy, I know that my grandmother would never — in a million years — agree to something like that." The truth was that DJ was secretly relieved for this excuse. The only thing she could imagine being worse than spending Christmas with Grandmother in Connecticut, or even her father's stepfamily in California, would be to spend Christmas in Las Vegas with Taylor Mitchell.

2

LOST IN LAS VEGAS

"WHY DON'T YOU JUST GO to the dance with Conner?" demanded Casey as DJ drove them home from school on Tuesday.

"I agree with Casey," said Taylor. "Why don't you just get it over with and say you'll go?"

"I agree too," chimed in Rhiannon. *"Just go,* DJ."

"You know you want to," urged Casey.

"Yes, I've admitted that," said DJ. "But I just don't want to risk hurting Haley again. She's been through so much already."

"That wasn't your fault," pointed out Rhiannon.

DJ knew that she hadn't been the one to push Haley into her "fake" suicide attempt—an attention-getting plan that nearly killed her. But DJ cared about Haley. She didn't want to take any chances.

"But you said that when Haley was in the hospital, she told you that she was fine with you and Conner getting back—"

"Sure, she said that. But who knows how she really felt? Or even how she feels now?"

"Where exactly is she now?" ventured Taylor.

"I'm not supposed to say."

"We know it's some kind of loony bin," said Taylor. "Why not just be honest and tell us?"

"It's *not* a loony bin." DJ scowled at Taylor as she stopped for the light. "If you must know, it's a therapeutic clinic in New Jersey."

"Tomatoes, to-MAH-toes. Same thing, Deej."

"Whatever. The point is I don't want to hurt her."

"I *know* what you're worried about ..." Taylor was using that sly tone she sometimes put on to get DJ going. "You think Haley's thugs are going to beat you up again, don't you?"

"I do not." Okay, that was a little worrisome. DJ had done what she could to befriend Bethany and Amy while Haley was still in the hospital. And while Amy showed some signs of understanding, Bethany (a very large and athletic girl) was another story. Bethany was fiercely loyal to Haley. So much so that DJ sometimes secretly wondered if Bethany had feelings beyond just friendship for Haley. Okay, that was ridiculous. But Bethany was scary.

"Why don't you just call Haley?" suggested Casey. "Ask her how she feels about it?"

"That seems a little harsh," pointed out DJ. "I mean, she's being treated for attempting suicide, and I'm calling up to see if it's okay if I go to the Winter Ball with the guy she OD'd for? Maybe I should ask her about my dress too, and, if I go for a white gown, is it okay to wear white shoes after Labor Day?"

"Yeah, that does seem a little harsh," agreed Rhiannon.

"So, really, you guys can give it up, okay?" said DJ. "I think Conner already has."

"I just feel sad that you're the only one in Carter House who's not going," said Rhiannon.

"Well, don't." DJ turned onto their street, eager to end this conversation. The truth was DJ felt a little sad about it. In fact, it seemed a little unfair. But it also seemed like the mature thing to do. As far as Crescent Cove High and the world at large were concerned, she and Conner were still just friends. And that's how she planned to keep it until she knew that Haley could handle it.

"So, do you think Rhiannon and I could borrow your car?" asked Casey. "We still have a few things to pick up for the dance."

"Sure ..." DJ pulled into the driveway, suddenly feeling even more out of it. "You mean this afternoon?"

"If you don't mind ..."

"We'd ask you to come along too," said Rhiannon apologetically, "but that might seem rude ... considering you're not going to the dance."

"Hey, why don't we all go," suggested Taylor suddenly. "You two can hit your retro stores, and DJ can help me pick out some really hot shoes."

"Okay," said DJ, actually feeling eager. "I'll just pretend like I'm going to the dance too."

"Who knows," said Casey, "maybe we'll change your mind."

"Or maybe just talk you into a new pair of shoes," teased Taylor.

So off they headed to the mall. For a while DJ pretended she, like them, was getting ready for the dance. She even held up some dresses and imagined she was going.

"Oh, DJ," said Taylor as DJ held up a garnet-red sequined number. "That is really hot." She shook her head. "And most people say blondes can't wear red."

"Well, I'm just a dishwater blonde," DJ reminded her.

"Why don't you just go?" demanded Taylor. "If it makes you feel better, send Haley a note to explain it. Sheesh, she's in therapy anyway. It might give her something to talk about during one of her group sessions."

DJ couldn't help but laugh. Still, it seemed mean.

"Seriously, DJ. You might be doing her a favor. Kind of a reality check. I mean, it's about time Haley figured out that, even though she tried to kill herself, she can't control other people. If a guy doesn't like you, he just doesn't like you. Get over it already."

DJ considered this. As harsh as it sounded, it was probably true. "I don't know ..."

"Look, DJ," said Taylor. "I know you're trying to be nice—the goody-good girl. But have you considered the possibility that you're just being codependent?"

"Huh?"

"You actually have some codependent traits."

"What do you mean?"

"Oh, your desire to keep everyone happy and—"

"I do *not* try to keep everyone happy."

Taylor laughed. "That's right. You usually try to make me miserable."

"I do not."

"See," said Taylor, like that proved her point.

DJ felt confused.

"All I'm saying is that you and Conner go tiptoeing around, pretending you're not dating so that you can protect Haley's delicate feelings while she's in the loony bin. And you think you're helping her? What happens when she's back in the real world and you and Conner, say, want to go to the prom? Do you blame yourselves if Haley gets hurt and goes and jumps off a bridge? Will you forever be responsible for Haley and the choices she makes?"

"That does sound a little creepy ... when you put it like that."

"It sounds unhealthy and codependent to me."

"So?"

"So, stop it!"

DJ pulled out her phone and hit Conner's speed dial. "Conner," she said in a firm voice, "do you still want to take me to the Winter Ball?"

"Of course."

So she quickly replayed what Taylor had just said, and Conner actually laughed. "Well, I can't believe that the room-mate from hell tells you what I've been saying to you for weeks, but you listen to her and not to me."

"Sorry," said DJ. "Sometimes God works in mysterious ways."

Taylor frowned at her with arms folded across her chest and toe tapping.

"Anyway, if you're okay, I'm okay," said DJ. "But I plan to write Haley a little note to let her know what's up. I think it'll just be kind of like an I'm-thinking-of-you sort of email, and then I'll casually mention that we're going to the dance next weekend. Does that sound okay?"

"I don't think you even need to do that much, DJ."

"I just want to."

"Yeah, that's one of the things I like about you."

She smiled. "Okay, then ... sounds like it's a date."

"You bet!"

"By the way, my dress is red."

"Right. Does that mean I need a red tux?"

DJ laughed and whispered to Taylor, "Conner just asked me if he needs to get a red tux."

Taylor snatched the phone. "Not red, you idiot." Then she told him specifically what he needed and where to get it before she handed the phone back to DJ.

"Sorry about that," DJ told Conner.

"No, it's actually helpful. But I probably should've been taking notes."

"I'm sure Taylor can write it down for you."

"Guess I can tell the guys to put me down for the stretch limo now. Harry's already ordered a Hummer."

"Sounds fun."

"I'm looking forward to it," said Conner. "This will be our first real date in a long time."

"Date?" DJ echoed, as the meaning of the word sank in.

"Well, it is, isn't it?"

"Yeah ..." she nodded slowly. "I guess so."

"And you're okay with that?"

"Yeah ... I'm just getting used to the idea."

"Have fun shopping."

"Thanks." DJ hung up and looked at Taylor. "I guess we're going."

"Of course you're going." Taylor shoved the red dress at her. "Now, try this on. I think it's your size, but I'll grab a couple of others just in case."

After several tries, DJ found the perfect fit. When she came out to show Taylor, a couple other shoppers paused to look. Everyone agreed that it was perfect. DJ spun around. "It feels so good to be in a dress like this without a big old cast on my foot."

Taylor laughed and explained to the bystanders that DJ had recently recovered from a broken leg.

"You look stunning," said the sales woman. "Do you want me to start writing it up for you?"

DJ paused. "Oh, I didn't even look at the price."

"Just put it on Granny's account," ordered Taylor.

"But I —"

"Trust me," said Taylor. "If necessary, I'll do the explaining. But I know that your grandmother would want you to have this dress, Desiree!"

"Yes, Desiree," said the saleswoman, "I'm sure she would."

But while Taylor was taking the dress up to the counter, DJ called her grandmother and quickly explained. "And Taylor insists it's the perfect dress," she said finally, "but I think it's a bit ex —"

"If Taylor says it's perfect, it's perfect," proclaimed Grandmother. "And I'm so pleased to hear you're going to the Winter Ball, Desiree. I didn't want to say anything or make you feel bad, but I was terribly disappointed when I heard you hadn't been invited."

DJ almost pointed out that she *had* been invited, but then she realized it would make no difference. Grandmother, as usual, would draw her own conclusions. Why bother? "Thanks, Grandmother," she said brightly. "And now I'll need shoes and —"

"Of course, you will. Ask Taylor to help you with those too. Her taste is as impeccable as her looks."

"Okay …" What Grandmother didn't know never failed to astonish DJ. Still, everyone knew that Taylor was Grandmother's prize pony.

"The secondhand store shoppers just called," said Taylor after the saleswoman put the dress on Mrs. Carter's account and handed over the sleek garment bag. "I told them the good news and that it'll take us at least an hour to snag the other things you'll need."

"They were okay with that?"

"Sure. Rhiannon said they'd just grab the metro back to town."

"They didn't mind using public transportation?"

"You know those two." Taylor shook her head. "The grittier it gets, the happier they are."

"Did they find what they're looking for?"

"Sounded like it." Taylor hurried DJ along. "And I just remembered seeing a great pair of shoes several shops back. I think they'll be perfect with that dress."

"Grandmother knew you would."

Taylor looked curiously at DJ and then laughed. "Well, of course!"

By the time they finished, DJ was starving. "Let's get something at the food court," she urged Taylor. "I'm craving real food."

Taylor looked like she was going to turn up her nose, but then she noticed the new Japanese place. "I could go for sushi."

"No," said DJ, pulling Taylor by the arm. "I mean real food. You've been bossing me around the fashion arena; I'm going to boss you around the cuisine arena. We're having pasta."

"Pasta?" Taylor's eyes lit up.

"Yeah. And, trust me, we've done enough walking and shopping that you don't need to worry about the calories."

So they didn't. As they sat there slurping up linguini with pesto, DJ thought there might be hope for them yet. After all, hadn't this been a fairly normal shopping trip? Just two friends out getting ready for the Winter Ball? Yet DJ knew

Taylor well enough to know that Taylor could pull the rug out from under her at any given moment. While that was kind of exciting—in an adrenaline rush sort of way—it was also a little frightening.

"SHOW AND TELL," said Eliza as soon as DJ and Taylor came into the house with their arms loaded up with bags.

"What?" Taylor frowned at Eliza.

"Come on," urged Eliza in her southern singsong voice. "Show and tell."

Taylor rolled her eyes. "In your dreams."

"But I showed you girls my dress on Sunday night," she protested.

"Showed off, don't you mean?" Taylor just kept walking up the stairs.

"Come on, DJ," urged Eliza. "Don't you want to show us your dress? We already know that you're going to the dance."

"Who told you?"

"Your grandmother," Kriti informed. "At dinner."

"So you've decided that Haley can just go take a flying leap?" teased Eliza.

"No. I realized that I was doing her no favors by sparing her from the truth." DJ looked up the stairs. Taylor was already in their room. "My roommate helped me to see the light."

Eliza laughed loudly.

Now Rhiannon and Casey looked down the stairs. "Did you find a dress?" called down Rhiannon.

"Yes, but she won't let us see it," Eliza called back up.

"I didn't say that."

"So, can we see?" asked Eliza hopefully.

"I'll think about it," said DJ. Then she ran up the stairs.

"We're watching a chick flick down here," said Kriti. "If you're interested."

"Thanks," said DJ. "But I have homework."

"And we're designing," called Rhiannon.

"So we've heard," Eliza called back. "Not that we're interested. Are we, Kriti? Who cares what everyone else in the house is wearing. We know that we'll look great."

DJ couldn't help but laugh as she went up the stairs. Why was it so vital for Eliza to know what everyone else was wearing? Of course, DJ knew the answer to this. It's like everything was a competition with that girl. A competition where Eliza Wilton had to come out on top.

DJ had already seen Eliza's dress. At first she thought it was a wedding gown. "So Harry decided to make you an honest woman," Taylor had teased. Eliza had just glared at her. But there was no denying the dress was pretty—in a confectionery sort of way. All sparkly white and fitted, and Eliza did look like a princess in it—albeit a Barbie princess. No surprises there since Eliza seemed to think she reigned.

And Kriti looked like a nice little lady-in-waiting to Princess Eliza. DJ thought the red gown didn't do much for Kriti's shape. Not that Kriti had a bad shape. But the velvet seemed heavy and awkward, and it didn't flatter Kriti who was much shorter than the other girls and not as slender. Mostly it seemed that the dress overwhelmed her. But Eliza had proclaimed it perfect. And for a handmaid, it probably was. Poor Kriti. Still, she seemed happy with her lot in life—catering to Eliza.

"Want a sneak peek?" whispered Rhiannon once DJ was at the second-floor landing.

"Of you guys?"

"Yeah, but we'd like to see your dress too."

"Sure." DJ slipped into their room, unzipping her bag to reveal the scrumptious gown.

"That's gorgeous," said Rhiannon with an affirming nod. "Really, really beautiful."

"Swanky," teased Casey.

DJ frowned.

"But pretty," Casey said quickly.

"Thanks. Now, show me what you guys put together." DJ looked around the messy room. Rhiannon's sewing machine was still out, and there were pieces of dresses and scarves and fabric strewn all about. "It's certainly interesting in here."

Rhiannon went over to her sewing machine and lifted up what appeared to be a pile of varying shades of green fabric. But when she held it up, it looked like an incredible creation. "What do you think?" she asked hopefully.

"I think it's fantastic, Rhiannon." DJ went closer to examine it. Although it was constructed of all different types of green fabrics, scarves, ribbons, beads, and trims, the dress didn't look goofy or homemade. "It's amazing."

"Isn't it?" said Casey with pride. "I can't believe she made this from scrap."

"From recycled dresses and blouses and whatever I could find that worked," said Rhiannon.

"You could sell clothes like this," said DJ.

"And you don't need to worry about anyone wearing the same dress," added Casey.

Rhiannon laughed. "For sure."

"Hold it up," urged DJ.

Rhiannon held it in front of her, and the rich green tones against her pale skin and vibrant red hair looked absolutely stunning.

"I can't imagine anything more beautiful," said DJ. "It's perfect."

"I told her she looks like a Celtic goddess," said Casey.

"It's certainly magical. It reminds me of Ireland ... or fairies."

"Thanks so much, you guys!" Rhiannon was beaming now. "It's kind of hard, you know, not having money like some people and trying to keep up with ... well, everyone."

"There's no need to keep up with me," said Casey.

"What are you wearing, Case?" DJ turned to look at her.

"Just like I said." Casey opened her closet and pulled out something that looked like a cross between a string corset and a multi-ruffled petticoat. "And I'll wear my black motorcycle jacket and fishnets and boots. You know, the rocking retro thing."

"Eliza's going to love this," teased DJ.

"I think that's why she's doing it." Rhiannon gave a slight frown. "Just to get Eliza's goat."

"And to express my individuality," proclaimed Casey.

"You'll both be one of a kind," said DJ. And a part of her wished that she'd used more ingenuity for her own gown. But, to be fair, creativity was not her strong suit. And she'd always been fashion-challenged.

As DJ zipped her gown back into the bag, Casey chuckled. "With you in that dress, Princess Eliza will probably be pea green with envy."

"I doubt that," said DJ. "But it's fun making her wait."

"Princess Eliza needs to learn that she doesn't rule Carter House," proclaimed Casey defiantly.

"Yeah," agreed DJ, "This isn't Eliza-lot."

Rhiannon laughed.

"Thanks for showing me your dresses." DJ headed for the door.

"You promise you won't show Eliza?" Casey peered at her.

DJ shrugged. "Don't know why I should."

Casey gave her a thumbs-up.

Of course, DJ felt slightly guilty. It's not like she specifically wanted to be mean or to exclude Eliza. But sometimes Eliza was so pushy. Oh, she'd do it in that sweet southern style. But it felt pushy all the same. Knowing that Eliza's parents were from one of the wealthiest families in the country didn't make it any easier to be nice. And, really, this *wasn't* Eliza-lot!

"Did you see Rhiannon and Casey's dresses?" Taylor asked with mild interest, not even looking up from her fashion rag.

"Yeah." DJ hung her dress in the closet. "Rhiannon's is spectacular."

"Really?" Taylor set the magazine aside.

"Like it-could-be-in-a-movie spectacular."

Taylor's brow creased slightly. "Maybe we should pay the girl to start designing for us."

DJ picked up her laptop and then sat on her bed. "You know, that's not a bad idea, Taylor."

"We'd have our own designer originals, and Rhiannon could make money for college."

DJ stared at Taylor in wonder. "Sometimes you blow my mind, Taylor."

Taylor looked surprised. "Huh?"

"You can be ... kind of mean sometimes ... and then surprisingly nice."

29

Taylor just shrugged, then returned to her magazine. "We all have our faults."

DJ laughed and opened her laptop. "I guess."

Before DJ started her homework, she decided to write Haley the promised note. She and Haley had emailed a few times (not daily) since Haley had gone to Oak View for treatment. After a few rewrites, DJ felt like the note had just the right tone to it. Light and encouraging, but honest and to the point. She read through it one more time.

Hey, Haley. I hope you're doing well. Life around here is pretty much the same. School is boring. Finals are impending. And everyone is counting down the days to Christmas break. Everyone but me that is, since all I get to do is stick around Carter House with my grandmother. Big thrill. I just wanted you to know (from me and not someone else) that I'm going to the Winter Ball with Conner next Saturday. The main reason I decided to go was because he felt left out since all his friends were going. And I suppose I felt left out too. I wish you were around so you could go too. I know there are dozens of guys who would jump at the chance to take you! And I hope it's not upsetting for you to hear that Conner and I are going to this dance together. I know you said that it's over between you two. But I don't want to make you feel sad. Catch ya later.

Love, DJ.

DJ said a quick prayer for Haley, then hit Send. Taylor was right, she told herself as she switched gears to homework. This might be one more step in Haley getting over it. And if it wasn't, well, wouldn't it be better for Haley to be where she had professional help anyway? Still, DJ decided this would be even more motivation to keep praying for Haley. She really did want her to get well—and soon. Hopefully Haley would be back to normal and back to school after winter break.

The next three days at school seemed focused on two things—the upcoming dance and complaining about finals. Kind of a dichotomy. By the end of the week, DJ realized that a lot of the talk and excitement wasn't only about the dance, but about what was happening *after* the dance.

It turned out—big surprise here—that some of the guys had rented some hotel suites in the same place where the Winter Ball was being held. And there was no mystery as to why they'd done this. Oh, sure, DJ had overhead guys saying things like, "We just want to keep the party going," or "we need a place to just relax and hang." But DJ was pretty sure she knew what it was all about. She mentioned this to Conner as they were going into the cafeteria for lunch on Friday.

"I'm assuming that you had the good sense not to rent a room?"

He looked shocked and then chuckled. "Well, I'm not a saint, DJ. But, no way! You know I would never do something like that."

"Besides being a waste of money, you'd end up dancing by yourself at the Winter Ball."

"Trust me, I know that."

She laughed. "Well, actually, I'm sure there are plenty of girls who'd want to dance with you, Conner. But I wouldn't be among them."

"Thanks." He grinned. "I got that."

"So what's up with these guys?" she said quietly, since they were getting into the lunch line now. "I mean, I even heard that Harry talked Josh Trundle into going in with them." DJ glanced to see if Kriti was around. "And I just can't imagine that Kriti would go for that."

"Unless Eliza talks her into it."

"Good point."

"And I'm sure you're aware that your roommate is on the guest list."

"Not that she's told me, but I assumed." DJ rolled her eyes as she picked up a tray.

"I heard that Garrison is in on it too. He and Seth reserved an adjoining suite."

Now this surprised her. "Does Casey know?"

Conner shrugged as he reached for a burger.

DJ sighed. "I wish our friends would just act like normal teenagers."

Conner laughed. "What's that supposed to mean?"

DJ had to laugh too. "I don't know ... I guess I just wish everyone wasn't so into playing grown-ups. Won't we get there soon enough?"

Unfortunately, Madison Dormont overheard this. And she laughed so loudly that she snorted. Then she took off, and DJ could only assume she ran to tell her friends. Not that DJ cared. Sometimes DJ wanted to shout her opinions from the rooftops. "Everybody just chill!" she would scream at the top of her lungs. "You don't have to drink alcohol or do drugs or have sex or break the rules to have fun in high school. News flash — it usually turns out to be exactly the opposite!" But DJ figured most kids wouldn't listen. Or if they were listening, they'd probably pretend they weren't.

Just the same, she decided to bring it up at Carter House. But not while her grandmother was listening.

They were just finishing up dinner. Grandmother had excused herself — she and the general were meeting for dessert, which was probably in the form of an after-dinner drink. DJ thought it was somewhat unusual that all six girls were still sitting around the table on a Friday night. But there wasn't a basketball game, or anything else it seemed, to tempt anyone besides Grandmother to go out on a cold blustery evening in East Connecticut. And DJ supposed, because of the big night planned for tomorrow, everyone was taking it easy tonight.

"So I hear some of the guys are planning an all-night party tomorrow," DJ mentioned casually.

"Are you coming?" asked Eliza.

"Thanks, but no thanks."

Eliza laughed. "I didn't think so."

"I'm curious as to how you explained this to my grandmother."

"What's that supposed to mean?" she asked.

"Nothing . . . just that I'm curious."

"You're not planning to rat on us, are you?"

DJ innocently held up her hands.

"I'm not completely sure that I'm going yet," said Kriti quickly.

"Good for you." DJ smiled at her.

"Yes," agreed Rhiannon. "That's the wise choice."

"Not that she's made up her mind," said Eliza with a cool smile.

DJ turned to Casey now. "So how about you?"

"What?"

"Are you joining in the all-night party?"

Casey shrugged. "I told Garrison we could go up there for a while."

"For a while?"

"Yeah . . . what's wrong with that?"

"What do you think is wrong with that?"

She shrugged again. "Nothing. We'll just hang and party awhile. Then I'll come home. No big deal."

"And do you honestly think that's why the guys are shelling out the big bucks to rent these expensive suites?" DJ asked her. "Just to put your feet up and have a few laughs?"

"Why not?"

"You don't think they expect anything in return?"

"Oh, DJ, lighten up," said Eliza. "Maybe we do just want to hang and have a few laughs. What is wrong with that?"

"What's wrong is that you know that's not what this is about, Eliza."

Taylor, who had been silently watching, had a sly grin on her face. DJ turned to her. "Tell them, Taylor. Why do you think the guys are renting hotel suites tomorrow night?"

"Why not?"

"See," said Eliza. "Even Taylor gets that it's no big deal. I don't see why you and Conner don't pop up to check on us if you don't believe it."

"Yeah, right." DJ glanced at Rhiannon for backup now.

"I have to side with DJ on this," she said firmly.

"What a surprise," said Eliza. "But, really, girls, if you're so sure that we'll be up there having some big orgy, why don't ya'll pay us a little visit?"

"Maybe we will," DJ said hotly.

Taylor laughed. "You will not."

DJ sighed in resignation. "Probably not."

"If it makes you feel any better," began Casey, "I'll lay my cards on the table with Garrison."

"Meaning what?" DJ challenged her.

"I'll tell him that if he's asking me up there to have sex, then he's out of luck."

34

DJ nodded. "I can actually imagine you saying that," DJ told her. "But I wonder if Garrison will take you seriously?"

"That's a good point," said Rhiannon. "It's like saying one thing and doing another."

"Like you tell a guy no and then you follow him up to his hotel room," DJ added. "What's that really saying?"

Casey seemed to consider this.

"I think Josh would understand," said Kriti quietly.

"I'll admit that Josh seems like a mature kind of guy," DJ told her. "But he's a guy."

"That's right," said Rhiannon. "I thought Bradford was more mature too ..." She glanced at Taylor, as did everyone else. "But I've been disappointed."

"All I'm saying," DJ said to everyone except Rhiannon, "is that if you go up to the suite with your boyfriends, no matter what they say, they will want things to go further."

"And, really," said Eliza in an exasperated tone, "is that any of your business, DJ?" She stood like she was leaving, and Kriti stood too, just like her puppet or puppy dog or lady-in-waiting.

"Because we live under the same roof and because some of you are my friends ... yeah, I think it is."

Taylor narrowed her eyes at DJ. "So what are you saying, DJ? Are you threatening to tell your grandmother? Because if that's the case, I will have my alibi ready."

"So will we," said Eliza. She was obviously speaking for Kriti too.

Casey said nothing.

"All I'm saying is that I hope you all use good sense tomorrow night."

"Your good sense?" asked Taylor. "Or our own?"

35

"Whatever." DJ rolled her eyes, wondering why she'd even bothered.

"Nice try," said Rhiannon after the other four had left.

"What's the point?"

"Do you think that's how God feels when he sends warnings to us?"

DJ sighed. "I don't know."

"Well, people have the right to make their own choices," Rhiannon reminded her, "and their own mistakes."

Although DJ knew Rhiannon was right, she still wished there was something she could do. Sometimes the only thing to do was to pray. And maybe that wasn't such a small thing.

4

"I DOUBT THAT ANY OTHER HOUSEHOLD in Crescent Cove has six young women under the same roof all getting ready for the same dance," said Grandmother at breakfast on Saturday morning.

"It's times like this that make me miss having my own bathroom back home," said Eliza longingly.

"Don't we all," said Taylor.

Grandmother got a thoughtful look. "However, this house does have six bathrooms."

"Yes, but not in our rooms," I reminded her.

"Well ..." Grandmother placed her forefinger on her chin. "I'm going to be out this evening ... so I suppose I could let someone use my bath ... and someone else could use the powder room downstairs." She chuckled. "But I doubt that Inez will volunteer her bathroom to anyone."

DJ laughed. "I doubt anyone would want to use it. I had the privilege when my leg was broken, and it's almost as big as a postage stamp."

"Still, that means all but two girls would have their own baths if—"

"I'd love to use your bathroom, Mrs. Carter," said Taylor quickly.

Eliza glared at her. "Well, then Kriti gets to use the powder room downstairs. At least I can have our bathroom to myself for a change."

"And I don't mind sharing." Rhiannon glanced at Casey.

"Me neither," said Casey.

"Miss and Miss Congeniality," said Taylor.

DJ knew it was silly to feel snubbed by Taylor's hasty claim on Grandmother's bathroom, but really, was she that hard to share a room with? It wasn't like living with Taylor was a walk in the park.

"Well, if you'll excuse us, Kriti and I have salon appointments," said Eliza as she stood.

"Have a good time getting pretty," said Grandmother. Then after they left, she looked around the table. "How about the rest of you? Are you getting hair or nails done today too?"

Rhiannon smiled. "We're playing beauty salon in our room. Casey's doing nails, and I'm doing hair." She glanced at DJ now. "Anyone interested?"

"I already made appointments for DJ and me," said Taylor quickly.

"What?" DJ frowned curiously at Taylor.

Taylor just smiled. "My treat, roommate. But you'll have to drive us there."

"What?"

"I made us appointments at Yobushi's."

"The new day spa that was in the paper last month?" said Grandmother, obviously impressed. "I heard they were booked for ages."

Taylor nodded. "Want to go, DJ?"

"Of course, she wants to go," said Grandmother. "And then you girls can come back and tell me everything about it tomorrow. I've been wanting to go myself, but I didn't think it was possible to get in."

"Maybe you should take my appointment," suggested DJ.

Grandmother laughed and waved her hand. "No, of course, not. You girls go and have a lovely time."

"Our appointments are for eleven," said Taylor. "But it's a forty minute drive to get there, so we should probably get ready."

DJ still wasn't sure, but with the encouragement of Grandmother and even Rhiannon and Casey, she figured why not? As they were heading upstairs, Eliza and Kriti were coming down.

"Guess where Taylor and DJ are going?" said Casey. It figured that Casey wouldn't be able to resist trying to bring Eliza down a notch.

"I can only imagine," said Eliza as she adjusted her bag.

"Yobushi's Day Spa," said Casey as proudly as if she were going too.

"Oh, sure," said Eliza. "I heard they were booked until summer."

"I guess it depends on who you know," said Taylor.

Eliza stopped and stared at Taylor, then smiled. "Maybe you only *think* you're going to Yobushi's, but you've actually booked an appointment at a sushi bar."

"Yes, maybe they'll give you a seaweed wrap," said Kriti.

DJ couldn't help but laugh. "Good one, Kriti."

"Or a wasabi facial," added Eliza.

"We'll get back to you on that," said Taylor lightly.

As it turned out, Taylor had gotten them appointments at the real Yobushi's, and DJ had never felt so pampered.

Between the elegant showers and the thick bathrobes and all the luxurious extras, DJ was starting to feel like a princess. "Have you done this before?" she asked Taylor as they were soaking in the hot tub following their facials and waiting for their pedicure/manicure appointments.

"Oh, sure, haven't you?"

"No . . ."

"So, you like it?"

"It's nicer than I expected."

"Everyone needs to be spoiled sometimes," said Taylor. "Even tough girls like you."

"You think I'm a tough girl?" DJ wasn't sure whether to be insulted or flattered.

"Well, you're the girl who jumps in front of SUVs to rescue kids. Then you do sports, swimming with a broken leg. I'd say you're pretty tough."

DJ sighed and leaned back into the tub. "Or maybe it's all an act."

"We're all actors . . . and the world is our stage."

"Is that Shakespeare?"

"Something like that."

By the end of the afternoon, DJ and Taylor emerged from Yobushi's feeling refreshed and beautiful. Not only did they have facials, pedicures, and manicures, but styled hair and makeup as well.

"I'll have to give Yobushi two thumbs-up," said DJ as she started her car. "Thanks for treating me, Taylor."

"You're welcome."

DJ glanced over at Taylor. She looked even more beautiful than usual, but she also had a sly little smile.

"Hopefully this wasn't meant to be some kind of bribe."

"No, of course not."

"If you were worried about me squealing to my grandmother about—"

"No, not at all. Even if you did, I can take care of myself. You know that."

"Yeah."

"Maybe I just wanted to be nice ... to keep you off balance."

"Why do you want to keep me off balance?"

"I was just kidding."

"Oh."

"And, just for the record, Taylor Mitchell doesn't allow any guy—no matter how much money he puts out—coerce her into having sex with him."

"Unless vodka is involved."

Taylor threw back her head and laughed. "Oh, DJ, one of these days, girlfriend, one of these days ..."

"What do you mean?"

"I mean one of these days you'll figure things out."

DJ wanted to question this. DJ would figure things out? How about Taylor? If anyone was mixed up, it was Taylor. But no one could tell Taylor anything. Taylor knew it all already.

"And another thing, DJ ..."

Hopefully this wasn't going to be sex advice.

"I do respect you for not having sex with Conner. I mean, if that's your choice, that's cool. But just don't go around forcing your morals and values on everyone else, okay?"

"Okay." The truth was DJ didn't want to force anything on anyone. But didn't she have the right to express an opinion? And to be fair, wasn't that what Eliza and Taylor did most of the time?

"You know what," she said to Taylor. "I just want to have fun tonight."

"Cool," said Taylor. "Me too."

DJ knew that their definitions of *fun* were as different as night and day. Although DJ did not get that, she decided not to think about it right now. Right now, she was feeling good. And tonight was going to be good. But before she stepped out with Conner in a few hours, she would check her email to see if Haley had responded yet. It was odd not to hear from her. Usually she wrote right back. DJ tried to convince herself this was not her problem. She was not responsible for Haley's emotional health.

"Do you know where the guys are taking us to dinner?" asked DJ as she exited the freeway into Crescent Cove.

"I do," said Taylor.

"Where?"

"If I told you, I'd have to kill you."

"Yeah, right."

"Well, it would spell trouble."

"What are you talking about?"

"It's supposed to be a surprise."

"I know, but how is it that you know? I thought it was something that Harry had cooked up."

"Yes ... you're almost right."

"Huh?"

Taylor laughed.

"Are you saying that Harry told you something?"

"I'm not saying anything, sweetie."

"So Harry told you where we're having dinner, but Eliza doesn't know?"

Taylor didn't answer, but DJ could tell by her smile that was the case.

"Why would Harry tell you and not her?"

"Maybe some girls can't be trusted with secrets."

"Why is it a secret?" demanded DJ. "What is going on anyway?"

"Don't get all hot and bothered," said Taylor. "It's no big deal."

"Well, what's going on?"

"Can I trust you to keep your mouth closed?"

"It depends."

"Okay, here's the deal. Harry's parents paid for a very nice catered dinner for all twelve of us at their beach house. The limo will take us there and then to the dance."

"Really?"

"Yeah. It'll be lots better than the local restaurants, which will be packed."

"That actually sounds kind of nice."

"Yes. I thought so."

"Why didn't he tell Eliza?"

"I told you, he wanted it to be a surprise."

"Oh . . ." DJ considered this. "Then why did he tell you?"

"He wanted some menu suggestions, and he knew I was a girl who *could* keep her mouth shut."

"Until now."

"You know how to keep your mouth shut too, DJ."

"Thanks . . . I think."

"Anyway, it should be a great meal. Harry's mom set it all up."

As DJ pulled into the driveway, she thought that at least the evening would start out nicely. What happened later on, after the dance ended, was anyone's guess. But at least she knew that she and Conner wouldn't be involved.

"Well, look at y'all," said Eliza. "Don't you look *pretty*!"

"Thanks," said DJ, and Taylor just smiled in a cool sort of way.

43

"So was it really Yobushi, DJ?" asked Eliza.

"It really was."

"And was it nice?"

"Oh, nice doesn't really describe it. Wonderful. Delightful." DJ sighed. "It was like a little slice of heaven."

Eliza blinked. "Well, sounds like you liked it."

"And now we have just enough time for a little nap," called Taylor from the stairs.

"Sounds good to me," said DJ.

But before she put her feet up, she checked her email. Still not a word from Haley. DJ decided to write her again. This time she didn't take as much care. But she didn't say anything untrue.

> Hi, Haley. Did you get my last email? It looks like it went through. But I haven't heard from you. Is everything okay? I can't imagine that you'd quit speaking to me because I'm going out with Conner. It's just a dance. It's not like we're engaged. Anyway, I really do care about you, and I hope you're okay. Please, write back. I'm praying for you to get well, Haley. But I know it won't help you for me to pretend that Conner and I don't like each other. So, if you need to, please talk to someone about this, okay?
>
> Love, DJ

Suddenly, DJ didn't feel quite so happy about the evening ahead. Oh, she knew it was silly to obsess over Haley's feelings. It's not like they made any sense. Not to a normal person. Still, it would've been a lot easier if Haley had written back. Even a brief, "Hey, it's okay … no problem … don't worry" would've been greatly welcome. As it was, DJ couldn't help but imagine Haley having a total meltdown over this. DJ wondered if she should call Haley's parents and tell them what was up. Or was that being codependent? Taylor would probably say, "Duh."

DJ glanced over to where Taylor was peacefully sleeping, flat on her back with her thick dark curls carefully arranged so as not to mess up her do. DJ wasn't even sure she could sleep like that. Maybe she couldn't sleep at all now.

So she just prayed. She prayed for Haley to be okay. She prayed for her housemates—and the evening ahead. She prayed that God would keep them safe and help them all to make wise choices.

AFTer a CHaoTIC Hour or TWO, all six girls, with five bathrooms between them, were eventually dressed to the nines. Eliza finally got to see what everyone else was wearing, and she made the predictable comments.

"Oh, Rhiannon," she said sweetly, "what an adorable gown. I almost wouldn't guess that you made it yourself." Then she turned to Casey. "No surprises here, Madonna. But it's Christmas not Halloween."

Casey smirked with her head held high as she clumped down the stairs with Rhiannon trailing gracefully behind her.

DJ frowned at Eliza, but continued to stand tall. Taylor had just given her a mini lecture about not slumping. "That dress deserves some posture," Taylor had said as she helped put the finishing touches on DJ's makeup.

"And you ..." Eliza scrutinized DJ now. "Well, the dress is obviously off the rack, but not bad."

"*Not bad?*" Taylor stepped forward and looked Eliza in the eyes. "DJ looks like a million bucks, and you know it. Why can't you just admit it?"

"And you, Taylor . . ." Eliza smiled slyly. "You will definitely stand out in the crowd."

Taylor held her head even higher. "Thank you, Princess Eliza. I will take that as a compliment." Then she linked arms with DJ, and they walked down the stairs. But about half-way down the stairs they overheard Eliza loudly whispering to Kriti.

"But if Taylor shows her fangs tonight, she might be mistaken for Vampira." As if on cue, Kriti laughed.

"Welcome to Eliza-lot," said DJ in a quiet voice.

Taylor threw back her head and laughed.

Then to everyone's surprise, Grandmother and the general met them downstairs and led them into the dining room where there was a tempting spread of appetizers.

"What is this?" asked DJ.

"General Harding insisted we see you girls off in style tonight," said Grandmother. "He even asked his cook to put together the hors d'oeuvres."

"And I shall play photographer," said the general as he focused his camera on DJ and Taylor. "Smile, beauties!" They smiled and he snapped.

"Very nice!" DJ smiled as she put a mini crab cake on her plate next to a deviled egg. Thanks to the general's cook, there was no low fat or low carbs going on here.

The general shot dozens of photos. Some posed, some candid. And when the guys arrived, things got even crazier—and louder. The guys looked as pleased to see the "treat" table as they were to see the girls. And the general soon began shooting photos of couples in the living room.

"Wow, DJ," Conner said as they waited to pose in front of the big fireplace. "You look incredible. Really awesome."

DJ smiled. "Thanks. Taylor was my fashion consultant."

Conner laughed. "As long as she's not your life consultant." They both turned to watch Taylor and Seth in front of the fireplace, hamming it up and even throwing in a kissing pose for the general.

"Yeah, right."

Soon the appetizers were picked over, the photos were shot, and it was time to go. The guys helped the girls with their coats and wraps and then escorted them out to where a white stretch Hummer was waiting.

"So where are you taking us?" chirped Eliza after they were all seated in the roomy limo.

"It's a surprise," said Harry with a twinkle in his eye.

DJ and Taylor exchanged glances, but apparently Eliza was watching.

"Hey, do you guys know where we're going?"

Taylor gave her the blankest of blank looks. DJ did her best to imitate, and then she turned to Conner and winked.

Of course, it wasn't long before they all figured it out, and soon they were piling out of the limo and into the well-lit beach house where fabulous seafood smells met them at the door. Candles were everywhere, and music was playing.

"Oh, Harry!" exclaimed Eliza. "You're a magician."

"You mean his mom is a magician," corrected Garrison.

Then Harry held up a cooler. "But my mom is not responsible for this."

"What's that?" asked Conner.

Harry put the cooler on the island in the kitchen. "Step up to the bar, folks."

DJ glanced at Conner, and he just frowned. Then she looked around the kitchen to see if any adults were around. Everything looked ready to go—the table was beautifully set for twelve, there were warming dishes and salads and breads all ready to serve. But no grown-ups.

"So your mom put this whole thing together and just left?" asked DJ.

Harry tossed DJ a questioning glance. "Is there a problem?"

DJ just shrugged. "Not with the food. It looks fantastic."

"Want to help put things on the table?" he asked.

"Sure," said DJ stiffly.

So DJ, Conner, Rhiannon, and Bradford put the serving dishes on the table. But once everything was set up—and even after DJ rang a fork on a glass as dinner bell, announcing "Dinner is served"—the others continued to cluster around the "bar." Casey kind of floated back and forth between the two different groups, but it seemed that Garrison still had his old pull and influence on her. Not for the first time, DJ wished that Casey had a different boyfriend. A nondrinking and respectful kind of boyfriend.

"Why am I not surprised?" asked DJ as she watched them refilling their glasses and toasting each other.

"So predictable," said Conner.

"Hopefully they'll still want to go to the dance." Rhiannon pointed to the oversized clock in the kitchen. "It's nearly eight now."

"Don't worry," said Bradford. "They've still got their suites to look forward to ... I'm sure we'll get to the hotel ... eventually."

"And the Hummer is waiting," pointed out Conner.

"I guess we could always eat and get the Hummer to take us back to town," added DJ.

"Why don't we sit down," suggested Conner. And so the four sat down, and Conner actually said a blessing.

"This food looks great," Bradford announced loudly, obviously for the sake of the others. "I guess we'll go ahead and get started."

DJ shook out her napkin. "Wow, lobster!" she said just as loudly.

"And don't blame us if there's nothing left," called out Conner. "Because I'm starving!"

Well, that seemed to get everyone's attention. They trickled over, carrying their drinks and finding seats at the table.

DJ had already decided not to make a scene. There really seemed no point. Like she'd said, why should this have surprised her? Still, it had caught her off guard. And it was disappointing. There seemed to be a silent agreement between the four nondrinkers to simply get through this. Before long, DJ assured herself, they would be at the dance.

But when they were finished with their meal, the others returned for another round of drinks, and Harry turned up the music so they could dance.

"Conner?" asked DJ from where they were sitting on the sidelines. "Can we go to the real dance before it's over?"

He nodded, then stood. "Okay, DJ and I are heading over to the Winter Ball now. And since I paid my share of the Hummer, we'll be taking the limo to get there." He kind of laughed. "But we'll be sure to send it back. Anyone want to join us?"

Naturally, Rhiannon and Bradford were ready to go. Then, to DJ's pleased surprise, Casey and Garrison said they were coming too. Although it sort of looked like Casey was dragging Garrison along.

"No one else?" called Conner.

"We'll be along later," said Harry lightly. "You kiddies have fun now." Then he scowled. "And don't forget to send the Hummer back."

"I don't see what the hurry is," said Garrison after the six of them were seated in the Hummer.

"We want to go to the dance," pointed out DJ. "Wasn't that the point?"

He shrugged, then slumped down into the seat.

DJ tossed Casey a look, but Casey looked the other way.

"Gee, this is fun," DJ said loudly to no one.

Conner frowned as if he was taking her comment personally. So DJ grabbed his hand and squeezed it. "Sorry, it actually *is* fun. But some people sort of take the thrill away. You know?"

He smiled now. "Yeah."

Across from them, Rhiannon and Bradford nodded. Then Rhiannon smiled. "But let's not let them, okay? We're still having fun despite the juvenile delinquents we left behind."

This made them all laugh. Well, except for Garrison. He looked rather glum and slightly sleepy. Or maybe he was just drunk. DJ wondered how much he'd had to drink. She also wondered, *What was the point?*

When they reached the hotel, Garrison looked a little unsteady as he attempted to get up from the seat.

"Hey, Garrison, you feeling all right?" asked Conner as he helped DJ get out of the limo.

"You look a little green around the gills, buddy," called Bradford as he and Rhiannon stood on the sidewalk.

Now Conner leaned back into the Hummer. "Need a hand?"

The four of them stood by the open doors to the Hummer, waiting for Casey and Garrison to join them.

"Come on," called Casey. "Let's get moving, Garrison."

"I don't ..."

Casey turned and looked into his face with a puzzled frown. "Are you feeling—"

Just then he hurled—blasting fragments of seafood and who knew what else all over Casey, himself, and the limo.

"Ugh!" DJ put her hand over her mouth and stepped back.

"Oh, that is so disgusting," said Bradford.

Just then the limo driver came running around, holding his hands in the air. "What is going on here?" he demanded. Then he looked in the back of the limo and let loose with a few foul words.

"Our friend is sick," said Conner. "Sorry about the mess." Then to DJ's amazement, Conner stepped back into the foul-smelling limo and helped Garrison out. And once outside, Garrison hurled again on the drive-around in front of the hotel. Not a pretty sight, as latecomers arrived for the Winter Ball, quickly sidestepping the nasty mess.

"You guys go on inside," said Conner. "I'll take care of Garrison."

"What about me?" Casey held her vomit-soaked layers of petticoat out and looked like she was about to cry.

"You kids are going to be charged for this mess!" yelled the angry limo driver. "No one's getting their deposit back!"

"Sorry about that," called Bradford. "Guess he was carsick."

"Carsick, my foot!"

"Don't forget that the people at the beach house still need you to pick them up," said Conner. "We paid for your service for the entire evening."

The man laughed now. "Oh, you'll get my service, all right. But you'll have to live with the smell."

Despite everything, DJ laughed as she imagined Harry and Eliza and the others' faces when they stepped into the limo.

Still, Harry had brought it on himself—he was the one who "opened up the bar."

"What am I going to do?" howled Casey.

"Let's get her to the bathroom," said Rhiannon.

"See you inside," called DJ to Conner.

"Let the good times roll," called Conner.

Getting chunks of barf out of layers of netting, laces on the corset, and not to mention the fishnet hosiery was no small challenge. Finally, Rhiannon and DJ just stepped back and shook their heads.

"There's no saving this outfit tonight," said Rhiannon.

"Why don't you take a cab home and change?"

Casey was crying now. "Yeah . . . I'll take a cab home, but I think I'll just stay there."

DJ didn't know what to say. "My guess is that Garrison might want to call it a night too."

"What a waste," said Casey as she threw the last of the soggy, smelly paper towels into the trash.

"Don't you mean *wasted*?" said Madison Dormont as she and Tina Clark emerged from where they'd obviously been listening in the lounge section of the ladies restroom. They both laughed, then stepping carefully, made their way to the mirrors where they checked their makeup.

"I hate to say I agree," said DJ. "But Madison is right."

"Thanks a lot," snapped Casey. She turned on the heel of her Doc Martin boot and stormed out with Rhiannon trailing behind her.

Then DJ went to the vanity to wash her hands and to touch up her own lip gloss. Remembering Taylor's lecture, she stood straighter. "But just for the record, Madison," she spoke slowly as she carefully coated her lips. "Casey wasn't the one who got wasted tonight. It was her boyfriend."

"If you sleep with swine," said Madison, "you wake up smelling like a pig." They both laughed as if they thought that was very clever.

DJ forced a smile as she mustered enough self-control not to say, "takes one to know one." Really, that would've been childish.

"Nice dress," said Tina as she snapped her evening bag closed.

DJ was surprised. "Were you talking to me?"

Tina shrugged, then nodded.

DJ smiled more genuinely this time. "Thanks. Yours is nice too."

"Thanks," said Tina with a cautious smile.

"Good grief," said Madison. "Aren't we having quite the little love fest in here. The guys are waiting, Tina."

DJ watched as Madison and Tina strolled out. Those two usually kept the enemy lines tightly drawn, but Tina had just let her guard down. Maybe if DJ made a little more effort, things could change. But for now, DJ had enough to deal with. She hurried out to see what had become of Casey and Garrison.

"There you are," said Conner as they met in the lobby.

"Where's Garrison?"

"He went up to the suite."

"Oh, that's right." DJ had almost forgotten the overnighter plan.

"Is he going to sleep it off?" asked Rhiannon.

"Actually, he sort of rallied after hurling all over the place," said Bradford. "He said he's going to change and hang around."

"But I put Casey in a cab to go home," said Rhiannon.

"Do you think she'll come back?" asked DJ.

"I don't know."

Bradford shook his head. "I'm sure Garrison will be giving her a call before too long."

"Hopefully she won't be answering," said DJ.

"Ladies," said Conner in a formal voice, "Are you ready to go to the ball?"

"Beyond ready," said DJ.

And so the four of them finally made it to the dance. Once inside, they danced and laughed and danced and visited with friends. DJ was reminded of how many good friends she had and how much fun it was to be with a big crowd like this. The band was actually pretty good. And the refreshments weren't bad either. All in all, she was having a great time.

"YOU'RE LIKE THE BELLE OF THE BALL," said Conner as he and DJ took a break near the punch table. It was nearly eleven, and DJ was finally feeling slightly tired. Still, it had been a great time . . . once they had made it into the ballroom.

"Yeah, right. But thanks anyway."

"Seriously, DJ. Everyone is looking at you."

She laughed. "That's crazy! They're probably just wondering where Eliza and Taylor are hiding." That's when she noticed the other half of their dinner party finally entering the ballroom. "Hey, look who just walked in."

Conner turned, and they both watched as Eliza, with Harry in tow, moved through the room. The couple looked slightly bedraggled, but Eliza's eyes were fixed on DJ as the two made their way to them. And if looks could kill, those icy blue daggers would've done the deed in seconds.

"Uh-oh," Conner said quietly. "Danger this way comes."

DJ forced a smile for Eliza. "Hello —"

"Save the greeting," hissed Eliza. She clutched DJ by the elbow and pulled her slightly away. But Conner came right along with her.

"Easy does it, Eliza." He smiled as he peeled Eliza's ice-cold fingers from DJ's arm.

"What did you guys do to the limo?" demanded Eliza.

"Huh?" DJ was confused. "Didn't it come back to get you?"

"Oh, yeah, it came back." Eliza glared at her.

By now the others had joined them. Kriti seemed almost as irate as Eliza, and Josh looked like he wondered what he'd gotten himself into. DJ could only imagine the newspaper story he might extract from this by next week. Harry looked only mildly irritated, probably because he'd had too much to drink. Seth looked ticked, but like he was trying not to show it. And Taylor actually looked somewhat amused—not to mention perfect with every hair in place. How did she do that?

"Who puked in the limo?" Eliza eyes were still fixed on DJ like she was personally responsible for the mess. "It smelled like—"

"It was Garrison," Conner said quickly.

"Yeah," added DJ. "He lost his cookies."

"And you couldn't have prevented that?" demanded Eliza. "You couldn't have asked the driver to pull over or stopped Garrison from throwing up all over the limo?" She pointed at DJ now. "You probably *made* him throw up!"

"We did not *make* him throw up!" DJ glared at Eliza with indignation.

"Garrison threw up because he'd had too much to drink." Conner directed this to Harry. "And if anyone's to blame, that would be you, Harry, my boy."

"Even so. You couldn't clean out the limo before you sent it back smelling like a cesspool?" Eliza once again directed this to DJ.

"Seriously, Eliza. You're acting like I'm the one to blame. What's up with that?"

"You guys are the only ones here. Who else do we blame?"

Just then Rhiannon and Bradford emerged from the dance floor and joined them. "What's going on?" asked Rhiannon brightly.

"*What's going on?*" Eliza aimed her venom at Rhiannon now. "You guys send us a freaking limo that reeks with the smell of—"

"Look, Eliza." Conner calmly stepped up to her. "If you have a beef, you should really take it up with dear old Garrison. He's the dude who hurled in the Hummer."

"And Casey," said DJ. "I mean he hurled on Casey too. She had to go home she was such a mess."

"Where is *dear old* Garrison anyway?" asked Harry.

"Upstairs in the suite."

Harry nodded. "I think I'll join him there."

"But we just got here." Eliza's voice was tightly pitched—kind of like a rubber band about to snap.

"So?" Harry looked blankly at his date.

"So, I haven't even danced yet, Harry."

He just shrugged. "So dance." Then with hands in his pockets, he just walked away.

"That's what I'm going to do." Taylor snatched up Seth's hand. "Let's boogy, baby!"

"Me too," said Rhiannon as she reached for Bradford.

"I'm with you guys." Now Conner grabbed DJ's hand, and Eliza was left standing with only Kriti and Josh for company. None of the three looked terribly pleased. No longer the ruling queen, Eliza looked more like a pouting princess with her scowling handmaid. And poor Josh looked like he wanted to make a fast break for the door. Who could blame him?

"I'd feel sorry for them," DJ told Conner as they started to dance. "Except that they brought it on themselves."

By the time the song ended, DJ didn't see Eliza anywhere on the dance floor. Her guess was that Eliza, tired of the humiliation of being dateless, had given in and gone upstairs to join Harry and Barf Boy. But she spotted Kriti and Josh sitting on the sidelines staring into space. Maybe they'd had too much to drink as well.

"It's sad," DJ said as she and Conner rejoined Rhiannon and Bradford between dances.

"What's that?"

"Oh, that people think adding alcohol to the mix is going to make things so much more fun and exciting." She nodded over to Kriti and Josh—the two bumps on a log.

"Wow, looks like they're having a great time," said Bradford sarcastically.

"And poor Casey is home alone," Rhiannon reminded them.

"And Eliza never got to dance once," said DJ. "Or to show off her princess gown." Okay, she hadn't needed to say that.

"Well, it looks like Taylor and Seth are enjoying themselves," observed Conner.

"So far ..." Rhiannon shook her head. "The night is still young for some people."

"Not for me," admitted DJ as the band leader announced the last song. "After this, I'm ready to call it a night."

"Me too," agreed Bradford.

"But do we have to ride home in that stinky Hummer?" asked Rhiannon.

Conner laughed. "Don't worry. I already arranged for a cab."

"Thanks for calling a cab," DJ told Conner as they went out for the last dance. "Thanks for everything tonight, Conner!"

And as she danced, DJ couldn't help but feel like Conner was the real deal. Tonight, when so many others were falling apart, he had stepped up and done his best to hold it together. He'd helped Garrison and stood up to Eliza. And all with a friendly sense of humor. Somehow he'd known how to make things right without making others feel particularly bad. DJ knew that wasn't her gift. She had a tendency to speak her mind no matter how it sounded. But maybe she could learn.

Conner and DJ were the first couple out of the cab, and that was fine with DJ. "It was a great night," said Conner as he escorted her up the walk to Carter House.

"In a weird and wild way, it was," she agreed.

"We sure have some messed-up friends."

"Unfortunately, that seems to be the case." They were on the porch now, still holding hands. "I have a feeling that I might choose different friends," she mused, "I mean some of them. But living under the same roof . . . well, it's tricky."

"Kind of like family."

"I guess . . . like a dysfunctional family." She knew they were making small talk. And she knew that this was that moment — to kiss or not to kiss. But she just wasn't sure. "But, hey, they kind of put the fun back into dysfunctional."

"You know what they say. You don't get to pick your relatives." Now he cupped her chin in his hands and looked into her eyes. "But if I were picking, I'd pick you for sure, DJ."

She smiled. "For a sister or a cousin?"

He laughed. "Not that kind of a relative."

"Good."

And then he kissed her. Just once. But it was a fairly long and solid kiss. And, really, once was enough. "Thanks," she breathed, reaching for the door handle behind her.

"Thank you!"

DJ let herself inside, quietly closing the door behind her. Okay, the evening hadn't been a complete success. But it hadn't been a complete mess either. At least not for her. But now she was concerned about Casey. Hopefully, she wasn't up there moping.

DJ went up and knocked on the bedroom door. When no one answered, DJ quietly opened it to see that the lights were already off. But enough light from the hallway showed Casey's soiled Madonna outfit piled in a corner and Casey snug in her bed. Probably sleeping off whatever it was she'd had to drink tonight. Poor Casey. DJ went over to check on her, but as she got closer, she realized that something about the form in Casey's bed didn't seem quite right. DJ jerked back the blankets to see that Casey had arranged pillows to look like her.

"What's up?" asked Rhiannon as she came in and turned on the light.

"Casey is gone."

"Gone where?" Rhiannon stared at Casey's rumpled but empty bed.

"Three guesses."

Rhiannon held up one finger. "Garrison called." Then another. "He begged Casey to come back to the hotel?" The third finger. "And she went."

"Bingo," said DJ sadly.

Rhiannon frowned. "She must've taken a cab."

"And now what?" DJ turned to Rhiannon.

"Guess that's up to Casey." Rhiannon kicked off her green velvet pumps and sighed.

DJ just shook her head. "Stupid. Stupid. Stupid."

As stupid as it was, there seemed to be nothing to do about it. But now DJ didn't feel sleepy. It wasn't so much that she was worried about Casey and the others. Just aggravated. She knew she could go and wake up Grandmother and tell all. But then what would Grandmother do? Drive over to the hotel and drag back Casey, Taylor, Eliza, and Kriti? Probably not. Certainly, she would be annoyed. And she'd probably give everyone another one of her "little lady lectures." But chances were that would be the end of it.

Except that everyone would be furious at DJ. Not that DJ cared so much. But she just wasn't sure what good it would do to stir the pot. Once again, it seemed the only thing she could do that would make any difference was to pray. At least she hoped it made a difference. Anyway, she prayed until she was so sleepy she thought even God must be getting weary of her words.

DJ WAS SURPRISED TO WAKE to the sound of Taylor snoring. Okay, she knew that Taylor only snored when she'd been drinking—heavily. But sure enough, when DJ turned over in her bed, she saw that the light in the bathroom was still on, and Taylor's gorgeous black dress was in a little puddle with her expensive shoes kicked off nearby. Now Taylor was sound asleep. Not soundlessly asleep. But she was definitely out.

DJ looked at the clock to see that it was 2:57. Not all that late, considering. Still, she wondered how long Taylor had been home ... or if anyone else had come back as well. But that could wait until morning. For now, DJ just wanted to sleep. Surprisingly, it came easier knowing that Taylor was safely home.

DJ didn't get up until ten, but Taylor was still asleep. Instead of stomping around, like she normally enjoyed doing when she felt certain that her roommate might be suffering a hangover, DJ tiptoed to the bathroom. She took a quick shower, pulled on some sweats, and then tiptoed downstairs where Rhiannon was sitting by herself at the breakfast table, her head bent over her economics book.

"Good morning," said DJ as she poured herself a cup of coffee.

"Hey, someone is finally up." Rhiannon smiled and closed her book.

"Did Casey make it back?"

"She came creeping in at about two thirty."

"Taylor's here too."

"I know. She helped to get Casey home."

"Helped?"

"Casey got into a fight with Garrison at the hotel. I think she'd had more to drink too."

"And?"

"And . . ." Rhiannon shrugged. "That's all I know. Taylor kind of helped her to bed and then filled me in . . . just barely."

"Really?"

"Taylor wasn't exactly sober either."

"I didn't think so."

"But apparently she was sober enough to call them a cab and get them back here."

"Taylor can function fairly well under the influence," DJ admitted. "I don't exactly know how, but I've seen it before."

"Good morning, ladies," said Grandmother as she joined them. "Where is everyone?"

"Sleeping off the big night, I expect," said DJ as she helped herself to a yogurt.

"So how was the ball?"

"It was wonderful," said Rhiannon.

"Yes," agreed DJ. "It was really fun. I had a great time."

"Oh, that's so nice to hear. I assume the other girls enjoyed themselves too."

"I'm sure they could fill you in on the details," said DJ. Although she was certain that was never going to happen.

Suddenly she was curious whether Eliza or Kriti made it home last night. She was also curious about her grandmother's reaction if they hadn't. On one hand, she didn't know if she cared if Eliza got caught. Grandmother would probably handle it herself without bothering to tell Eliza's parents. But it might go differently with Kriti. DJ knew Kriti would be crushed if her parents found out what she'd been up to. On the other hand, maybe it would help Kriti if her parents knew what was going on.

Whatever the case, DJ sneaked up to check on their room after breakfast and was relieved to see that Kriti was there and just getting up.

"Sorry to bother you," said DJ. "But my grandmother was asking after everyone, and I was curious if you made it back okay."

Kriti nodded and rubbed her head as if it was aching.

"And Eliza too?"

"No," said Kriti hoarsely. "She stayed over."

"Oh."

"I came back with Taylor and Casey."

"Were you glad to come back?"

Kriti sighed. "Yes and no."

"Huh?"

"I was relieved to get home and sleep in my own bed. But Eliza will be mad when she finds out."

"She didn't know you left?"

"No."

"Oh." DJ considered this. "Well, you shouldn't allow Eliza to push you around so much. She's not your—"

"She's my best friend," Kriti declared stubbornly. "If you'll excuse me." Then she hurried to the bathroom. DJ hoped she wasn't about to throw up, because she did look rather pasty.

DJ sighed and returned to her room to fetch her homework and laptop. Like Rhiannon, DJ wanted to spend part of the day studying for finals. But she planned to squat in the library, where she could study in undisturbed privacy. She wouldn't admit it to her roommates, but she was getting a little tired of all of them. In fact, as far as DJ was concerned, winter break wouldn't get here quickly enough. She knew she needed a break. And she suspected she wasn't the only one.

By dinnertime, all of the Carter House girls were present and accounted for. Grandmother, pleased to see the additional four, questioned them about last night's ball. And their slightly unenthusiastic answers were predictably dishonest. Not that Grandmother seemed to notice or care. Sometimes DJ felt her grandmother simply created her own reality—a shallow, superficial kind of reality that barely scratched the surface. Still, it seemed to make her happy.

"Where have you been keeping yourself all day?" asked Taylor as they were finally getting ready for bed.

"Studying for finals." DJ peeled back her comforter and slipped between the sheets.

"Yeah, right."

"I *was* studying," DJ defended herself as she reached to turn off her bedside lamp. "I happen to care about my grades."

"Whatever."

"Seriously, Taylor. I *was* studying. I was in the library for most of the day. Is that a crime?"

"No."

"I actually thought you might appreciate the privacy."

Taylor didn't say anything, just continued her meticulous process for getting ready for bed. This meant the application of various creams and lotions and ointments, and DJ wondered how a person could possibly keep track of all those beauty products and what they were meant to be used for. And what would happen if Taylor accidentally put eye ointment on her elbows or foot cream on her face? Would she wake up looking like the Bride of Frankenstein?

"So are you saying you missed me?" DJ grinned as Taylor looked up from rubbing something green onto her heels.

"In your dreams." But Taylor was smiling now. "I just didn't want to feel like I ran you out of your own room."

"That wasn't it," DJ protested. "And, if I remember correctly, you're the one who leaped at the opportunity to have a private bathroom yesterday."

Taylor chuckled. "That was just to beat Eliza to the punch."

"Good one."

"So, really, you're not mad at me?" asked Taylor.

"Mad at you?"

"For last night."

"What do you mean?" DJ was trying to remember if Taylor had done anything to offend her last night. Eliza sure had.

"You know, for the drinking and all."

DJ shrugged. "Okay, I wasn't too thrilled with that crud. But that's no surprise, right?"

Taylor shrugged.

"I mean, it's not like you did anything to me personally. And it was nice of you to help Casey and Kriti get home."

"Somebody had to."

"And Eliza probably wasn't offering."

"I think Eliza was snot-faced drunk by then."

"She was drunk?"

"Yes. She came up to the suite and started laying into Harry. It was actually kind of amusing in a disturbing way. I'd never seen sweet Eliza lose her cool like that. We were all pretty stunned. I think she'd already had so much to drink that it loosened up her tongue. You know what they say."

"What?"

"Being drunk just brings out the real you. If you're a goof-ball, like Harry, you just get goofier. If you're a witch like ... well, watch out."

"So Eliza was acting a little witchy?"

Taylor nodded and sat down on her bed. "Harry was being all sweet and nice, trying to calm her down, telling her how pretty she looked, how she was really the queen of the ball." Taylor laughed.

DJ just shook her head.

"Because that's what Eliza was really mad about. She was going on about how she didn't get to dance on center stage and hog all the attention. She didn't say it quite like that, but we all knew what she meant."

"I can just imagine."

"But good old Harry just kept placating her and pouring drinks into her. Before long, she was snookered."

"Lovely."

Taylor rolled her eyes. "Tell me about it."

"So you brought Casey and Kriti back? Did the other guys all stay at the hotel?"

Taylor laughed. "Like Eliza spent the night with four guys?"

"Not seriously?" DJ blinked.

"No. At least I don't think so." Taylor suddenly frowned. "Anyway, that better not be the case." She shook her head like she was trying to piece it together. "No. For one thing, I think Seth planned to leave too. At least that's what he said."

"Was he okay with you leaving?"

"Are you kidding?" She laughed. "But that's his problem. If I think it's time to go, it's time to go."

DJ gave her a thumbs-up.

"And, come to think of it, Josh was heading out too." Taylor yawned and switched off her bedside lamp. "And that's all she wrote."

They said good night, but DJ suddenly imagined Eliza intoxicated and alone in the hotel suite with four guys. Then she told herself that it was probably only two guys. Still, it was messed up. Despite her other harsh feelings, DJ felt a little sorry for Eliza. Why would she put herself in that situation? Why would she allow herself to be that vulnerable? That helpless? Because she was too drunk to know the difference? Duh. And just the idea of this made DJ feel slightly sick. So she prayed for Eliza. Of all six girls at Carter House, she might've been more in need of prayer than anyone.

Finals week dragged on . . . and on and on. When it was finally over, a lot of kids were gathered at McHenry's Coffee House, saying their winter-break farewells.

Conner and DJ were at a corner table, exchanging Christmas cards, which they weren't supposed to open until Christmas. "We can only do cards," DJ had told him earlier in the week, after they'd overheard others talking about the expensive gifts they were getting for each other. DJ suspected that Eliza would receive diamonds from Harry (in an effort to make up for last weekend, which had been totally glossed over — naturally).

"I wish I could stay longer," Conner said, glancing at his watch. "But we're doing a red-eye flight, and I still have some packing to do."

"I understand." DJ smiled. "Although I'll miss you."

"I'll miss you too."

She laughed. "Yeah, you'll be having the time of your life on those slopes and—"

"We won't be on the slopes the whole time," he reminded her. "Don't forget we have to visit Aunt Ginger."

She smiled. "Yes, Aunt Ginger . . . the woman with a cleaning fetish. Well, that should be fun."

"You walk into her house, and all you can smell is bleach and disinfectant," he said. "I swear you think you've just entered a crime scene that someone has already scrubbed down."

"Maybe that's it," DJ said slyly. "Maybe Aunt Ginger is really a serial killer just covering up her tracks."

"I will miss you!" Conner leaned over the table, DJ leaned to meet him, and they kissed. Then Conner slowly stood and said good-bye before he pressed his way through the crowded coffee house.

"There goes Prince Charming," said Taylor as she carried her coffee over and sat next to DJ. "Where's he off to?"

"Montana." DJ sighed as she watched him going out the door.

"Skiing?"

DJ nodded. "And solving murder mysteries."

"Huh?"

"Nothing." DJ brought herself back to reality. "Where's Seth?"

"He had to go to some family Christmas party."

"And he didn't ask you?"

"I need to go home and pack. My flight's an early one. Hey, speaking of that, how about a ride to the airport?"

DJ frowned. "How early?"

Taylor shook her head. "That's okay. It's really early. I'll just call a cab."

"No, I'm sorry," said DJ quickly. "What time?"

"I'll need to leave the house by six."

DJ shrugged. "That's not so bad."

"You sure?"

"Yeah. And about the time I get back, it'll be time to take Rhiannon to the train station."

"What are you, the Carter House cab?"

"Grandmother already offered to take Eliza and Casey. Their flights leave about the same time."

"And then it'll be just little old you … alone with your grandmother."

DJ nodded with a flat expression. Okay, she wasn't about to admit that she was looking forward to being alone. Not so she could be alone with Grandmother. She simply wanted to enjoy being alone. Not sharing a bathroom. Not hearing Taylor snore. Not putting up with Princess Eliza. Not listening to Casey pick fights. DJ just wanted to be alone. And, although she wouldn't let on to anyone, it was going to be delightful. Luxurious. Relaxing. Like a much-needed vacation from noise, chaos, and clutter. She couldn't wait!

8

LESS THAN A WEEK INTO WINTER BREAK, DJ didn't think
she could survive Christmas. It wasn't Christmas as much as it
was rattling around by herself in the big empty house. Just one
day after the other girls vacated, the quietness had started to
get to DJ. She couldn't even believe it at first. She told herself it
was probably kind of like culture shock. She just needed to get
used to it. But days later, she was seriously lonely. She missed
her roommates. And it was hard to admit, if only to herself,
but she missed Taylor most of all. How weird was that?

"Desiree?" called Grandmother as she knocked on the bedroom door.

"Come in." DJ looked up from where she was sitting in the
window seat, checking email on her laptop. Haley had just
gotten back to her. She claimed that she'd been too busy to
answer before, but said that it was no big deal if Conner and
DJ were going out again. DJ wasn't convinced.

DJ closed her laptop as Grandmother entered the bedroom.
DJ didn't usually take that much interest in her Grandmother's appearance or mannerisms, but today she watched with
hungry interest as Grandmother tossed a tail of her pale blue

scarf over one shoulder. DJ's nose took in the smell of Grandmother's expensive perfume. And she even glanced down at Grandmother's sleek platinum pumps. It wasn't that DJ was into fashion—especially old-lady fashion—she suspected she was simply missing her friends.

"The general has invited us to join him for dinner again tonight, Desiree. He just called to say that some old friends dropped by with a crate of the most lovely lobsters, and they need help eating them."

DJ frowned slightly. Not that she didn't enjoy the general's company—at times. But this would be the *third* time since Christmas break that she'd have spent an evening with him and Grandmother. It was getting old already.

"I think I'll pass," she said quietly. "Thanks anyway."

Grandmother nodded and actually seemed relieved. Perhaps she too was getting weary of her tagalong granddaughter—the third wheel. "All right. I'll tell Clara to fix you some—"

"No," DJ said quickly. "Don't make Clara stick around for me tonight. I'll forage something for myself." No way did DJ want to be responsible for Clara grumping around the kitchen when she could've had the night off. It just wasn't worth it.

"Well, okay then." Grandmother patted her sleek silver hair and smiled. "If you're sure ..."

"I'm sure. And do thank the general for me." DJ held up a book that she'd started a couple of days ago. "I'd like to finish this tonight anyway."

Grandmother reached for the door. "Have a good evening then."

"You too."

DJ looked back at her email box, wishing that something new had popped up, but it was just the same. And why not? Other people had things to do, places to go, and people to see.

She was the only one without a life. Maybe she should have gone to visit her dad and stepmom and twin half sisters. Dad had even called to invite her again just a few days ago.

"Sally and Callie are just starting to talk," he'd told her cheerfully. "It'll be the first Christmas to know what's going on." Like DJ cared. Okay, she knew that sounded all wrong—it wasn't as if she hated the little girls. But perhaps she did envy them a bit—and maybe even more now that it was Christmas and she was lonely. But her intuitions were stronger than ever that if she gave in, her stepmom would assume that DJ was a built-in babysitter. Not.

DJ shoved her computer aside and picked up her book, trying to focus on the words, but her mind was not into it. Home alone on a Friday night, reading a book—how pathetic. Still, she was determined not to feel sorry for herself. And, really, she was happy that her friends each had something pretty cool to do for Christmas break.

Eliza was probably having fun in Kentucky right now, and before long she'd be off to France to join her parents at their restored vineyard estate. And even though Kriti wasn't that far away in New York City with her family, she had "a couple dozen relatives" coming to visit from Delhi. DJ couldn't imagine having that many relatives, but at the moment, it sounded wonderful. And Casey was home in sunny Southern California, where her parents were enormously relieved to see that she was looking and acting more like her old self again. She'd emailed DJ to say how they had credited Grandmother for this amazing transformation. DJ wondered what they would've thought if they could've seen Casey at the Winter Ball, dressed like Madonna and covered from head to toe in her boyfriend's vomit. Even Rhiannon had been excited about Christmas break. It turned out that her mom did get released from her drug rehab program. And she was going to be out for a full week—released to the "custody" of the elderly aunt in Maine. Hopefully Rhiannon's mom wouldn't fall off the wagon.

"Please, pray for her, DJ," Rhiannon had asked when DJ had dropped her at the train station last week. Naturally, DJ had been praying.

DJ was jarred back to reality by the jingling of her cell phone. She wished it would be Conner, but doubted it since she knew cell phone service was sketchy where he was staying. To her surprise it was Taylor.

"Hey, girlfriend," said Taylor cheerfully.

"Hey, Taylor! It's so good to hear your voice!" Of course, DJ instantly regretted this gushy-sounding response. She didn't want Taylor to know how much she missed her—or just how lonely she really was right now. Not cool.

"What's up?"

"Not much. Where are you?" The last DJ had heard, they'd been in New Mexico, but that was a few days ago.

"We're on our way to Las Vegas, baby." Taylor laughed. "We just left Phoenix about an hour ago."

"How's the weather down there?" asked DJ.

"Sunny ... warm ... just about perfect."

"Sounds lovely. It's been cold and wet and windy here. You'd think it could at least snow."

"Ugh, that sounds nasty. Too bad for you, Deej." Then Taylor chuckled in the low-pitched way that she sometimes used when planning mischief. "I'll think of you while I'm lounging out by the pool, sipping a frosty margarita."

"Your mom doesn't mind you drinking?" DJ was actually curious as to how Eva Perez felt about her daughter's wild habits. Maybe she didn't care.

"Oh, it'll be a *virgin* margarita, of course."

"Of course."

"The hotel has like six pools."

"How long are you staying there?" asked DJ wistfully—or to be honest it was probably enviously. Had Taylor called just to rub it in, to remind DJ that her life was probably the most boring one on the planet?

"My mom's booked there until New Year's. She's performing in one of those megahotels—you know the kind that has everything you could possibly want all under one roof. Well, I guess it's not exactly one roof, but you know what I mean. I just checked it out online, and it's got the best designer shops and restaurants and a really great spa."

"Cool."

"Totally. And, trust me, anything will be an improvement over this stuffy old bus. The bathroom in here is about the size of a bathmat. I can't wait to get out and stretch my legs. Sin City, here I come!"

"Sounds like fun." DJ sighed. Okay, maybe the Sin City part didn't sound like fun. But the pools and sunshine and spa sounded a lot better than being stuck in Crescent Cove, Connecticut—with about half the town's population evacuated for more adventurous locations.

"Hey, why don't you join me down here, Deej?"

DJ laughed with sarcasm. "Yeah, right."

"Seriously," said Taylor. "I'm sure my mom wouldn't mind, and we're supposed to have a big suite with two separate bedrooms. You could room with me if you want."

"Really?" DJ was amazed at this generous offer. "Are you serious?"

"Totally. In fact, my mom would probably love it if you came down," said Taylor. "Just this morning she said she feels guilty that I'm on my own so much. Not that she can help it.

She performs every night, then has to rest in the mornings. And then she has rehearsals almost every afternoon."

"That sounds exhausting."

"I think it is. Anyway, I'm sure she'd like you to come, DJ. She'd probably think you're a good influence on me."

"She thinks you need a good influence?"

"That's practically what she said the other day—she caught me flirting with a guy at the gas station."

"A guy at the gas station?" DJ shook her head. "That sounds a little desperate."

"What can I say? He was totally hot. Seriously, he looked just like Usher."

DJ laughed.

"So how about it?" persisted Taylor.

"I don't know . . . I mean if I actually did come, would it be to babysit you and keep you out of trouble?"

Taylor laughed loudly. "Yeah, like that's going to happen. Get real, DJ. Do you honestly think you could keep me out of trouble?"

DJ considered this. Being with Taylor in a place like Las Vegas could be a serious challenge at best. And yet . . . the idea of getting away to someplace warm and doing something fun. Well, it was tempting. And maybe Taylor's mom was right . . . maybe Taylor did need a good influence. Maybe DJ would be doing a good deed. Or not.

"Ask your grandmother," urged Taylor. "Tell her that I begged you. Tell her that I'm lonely and need my roommate."

DJ couldn't believe she was actually considering it. "This is crazy."

"Crazy good," said Taylor. "Come on, I need you down here with me. It's not fun dressing up and strutting around all by myself. Come on, DJ."

"My grandmother will never agree to it."

"Go ask her!" commanded Taylor. "Right now."

"What about your mom?"

"I'll check with her too. But, honestly, she'll probably be thrilled. And if it'll help, I can have her call Mrs. Carter for you."

"Okay, I guess it can't hurt to try." But even as she said this, DJ wondered if the idea was totally nuts.

"Call me right back, okay?"

"My grandmother might be gone by now. She's having dinner at the general's tonight and—"

"Quit talking and start moving!" Then Taylor hung up.

DJ braced herself as she walked down the hall toward Grandmother's suite. Grandmother was probably gone anyway. And if she was still here, surely she'd never agree to anything like this. It was outrageous! Two seventeen-year-old girls practically unsupervised in Sin City. Even Grandmother could see the potential problems with that little setup. Still, for Taylor's sake, DJ knew she had to ask. Then she'd call Taylor and act disappointed that Grandmother had denied her request, saying that she'd given it her best shot.

DJ paused at Grandmother's door. She could hear her voice chattering away with an excited edge to it, probably talking to some big-shot fashion friend on the phone. So DJ waited, but as she stood there, she shot up a quick prayer, asking God to intervene and to direct her grandmother's answer in regard to Vegas, which convinced DJ that the answer would most likely be a big fat no. It took a couple of minutes for Grandmother to finally get off the phone. Then DJ knocked and waited until Grandmother opened the door with a big smile.

"I need to ask you—"

"Oh, Desiree," gushed Grandmother. "I'm so deliriously happy. That's the most wonderful news!"

DJ was confused now. "Did Taylor's mom already call you?"

Grandmother blinked, then shook her head. "No. That was my designer friend from New York. Remember how Dylan was so impressed with you girls at the Founder's Day Fashion Show? Well, other than that little fiasco between Eliza and Taylor, which actually turned out to be a rather smart publicity stunt—at least that's what Dylan thought it was. Anyway, he has invited all you girls to come to New York for Fashion Week the end of January. The Carter House girls will be modeling his new fall line."

"A fall line in January?"

"Well, of course. It's always shown in late January or early February, Desiree."

"Of course."

"That gives the buyers a chance to plan for the fall season, which actually begins in early summer."

DJ tried to wrap her head around those conflicting seasons. "Right . . ."

"But what's this about Taylor's mother?" Grandmother frowned. "Is something wrong?"

"No. Nothing's wrong. But Taylor just called—you know she's touring with her mom during the holidays."

"Oh, yes. How is our beautiful Taylor?"

"Lonely."

Grandmother's brow creased ever so slightly. Her recent Botox injections must be doing their magic. "Taylor's lonely?"

"Yes. It seems her mom is busy with the tour, and Taylor is on her own a lot."

"Well, naturally, Eva must be very busy . . . so very much in demand. She's such an amazing woman . . . so talented."

"Anyway, Taylor called to ask if I could come join them in Las Vegas."

Grandmother looked surprised. "Las Vegas?"

"Her mom is performing in some huge hotel, and they'll be staying there until New Year's. I guess they have a big suite with plenty of room for me to join them, and Taylor really wants me to come."

"Oh, my . . ." Grandmother pressed a perfectly manicured fingertip to her chin. "Las Vegas. Why, this is so sudden."

DJ nodded. "I know. Taylor said that her mom can call you . . . if you like."

"Goodness." Grandmother sat down in a cream-colored armchair and just shook her head. "I'm not sure what to say."

Suddenly DJ wanted her grandmother to agree to this slightly insane plan. She couldn't even explain why, since part of her questioned the whole thing. Yet another part wanted to go. "Taylor asked me to beg you," persisted DJ. "She said she really, really needs me down there."

Grandmother nodded. "Poor Taylor. Yes, I can understand that. She is such a beauty . . . and she is so easily confused. She needs a girl with your mature sensibilities to help her along."

DJ tried not to look too surprised by this statement, since Grandmother never described DJ as mature or sensible. Beyond that, it was ludicrous to think that DJ or anyone else actually had much influence over someone like Taylor. Still . . . it was nice that Grandmother thought so.

Grandmother glanced at her diamond-encrusted wristwatch. "Goodness, it's almost time to go to the general's."

"Do you want Taylor's mom to call you?"

"Yes ... in fact, you can have her call me at the general's." Grandmother smiled coyly. "That will be quite impressive, you know, for me to receive a call from the talented Eva Perez in front of the general's friends."

"And what should I tell Taylor in the meantime?" asked DJ.

"That you are coming, of course!"

Shocked, DJ pressed her lips together.

"Well, as long as Eva is in favor of this little plan. If it's something that you and Taylor cooked up yourselves ... well, I'll be very disappointed in you, Desiree."

"I can't speak for Ms. Perez," said DJ quickly. "But Taylor seemed to think she'd be happy for Taylor to have a companion."

"Perhaps the general can help with your travel arrangements. He seems to know how to do these things on the computer. He told me that he rarely relies on travel agents anymore." Grandmother paused from pulling on her fur-trimmed coat. "But, Desiree, this means you won't be here for Christmas."

DJ considered this. "Will you be okay?"

"Oh, certainly. The general had already invited us to join him for a pheasant dinner." She reached for her bag—a very expensive Bottega Veneta that Taylor often lusted over—and slipped it over her arm. "But now I suppose it will be only the general and me."

"I hope you don't mind."

Grandmother smiled. "Not at all, Desiree. And I actually think it's lovely that you want to help our poor Taylor like this. She is such a beauty—and she'll be such a necessity to our big debut during Fashion Week—you must be sure to keep her safe and sound in Las Vegas. Bring her back to Carter House in one piece, dear."

DJ nodded without answering. Was that the only reason Grandmother was agreeing to this totally outrageous idea — because she wanted DJ to go out to Sin City to act as Taylor's bodyguard? Just to ensure that Taylor would be around to participate in Fashion Week? Talk about bizarre! Suddenly, DJ wondered what she was getting herself into.

"GOING HOME FOR THE HOLIDAYS, DEAR?"

DJ looked up from her paperback to see a white-haired woman seated next to her and smiling hopefully. DJ was sitting in the O'Hare terminal now, waiting for her next flight—to Las Vegas—which was running two hours late. "You mean me?"

"I'm sorry to interrupt your reading," apologized the woman. "But I'm just dying to talk to someone."

"That's okay." DJ stuck her boarding pass in the book as a marker and smiled back at the woman. "Now what did you ask me?"

"Are you going home for Christmas? Does your family live in Las Vegas?"

DJ frowned. "Actually I'm going out there to meet a friend."

The woman looked slightly surprised. "Oh ... you're meeting your friend for the holidays?"

DJ made a slight nod.

"Not going home to be with your family then?"

"I don't exactly have that kind of family." DJ wasn't sure how much she wanted to say.

The woman waved her hand. "Oh, you'll have to excuse me, dear. My daughter is always telling me I'm far too nosey. I just assumed you were a college girl on her way home for Christmas vacation. My son lives in Las Vegas, and I'm going to spend the holidays with him and his family. My grandchildren are all grown-up like you, but I'm hoping that some of them will take time to pop in and visit us while I'm there."

DJ considered telling this woman that she was only seventeen, but then wondered why bother? Besides, she was sort of flattered that the woman assumed she was in college.

"I must say I'm looking forward to some sunny weather. I heard that they're having quite a nice warm spell in Las Vegas."

"Yes, my friend said it was supposed to get into the low eighties today."

"Goodness, that is warm." The woman peered out the window where snow was flying. "Not like here." She shuddered. "I just hope we don't get stuck."

"Stuck?"

"Well, we could be stuck if this storm doesn't let up. I heard they're having a hard time keeping the runways cleared. They hadn't expected this much snow."

"Is that why we're delayed?"

"That's what I heard. I just hope we're not stuck here all night."

"All night?" Now DJ was feeling concerned.

"Yes, it happens a lot here. The weather gets so bad that the flights are cancelled. And at this time of year, it's nearly impossible to get a hotel. I know because it happened to me a couple of years ago."

"What did you do?"

The woman smiled and shrugged. "Made the best of it."

DJ groaned.

"Now, if an old woman like me can make the best of it, surely you should have no problem."

"I guess . . . but the idea of spending the night in a crowded airport doesn't exactly sound fun."

"Think of it as an adventure."

DJ looked out at the swirling snow and wondered if it had been a mistake to come. The plans had all seemed to work out smoothly. Grandmother had a nice conversation with Taylor's mother. The general had been successful at booking the flight, which he said was nothing short of miraculous at this time of year. So DJ had assumed that this was God's way of giving her the green light. But maybe she'd been wrong.

"I learned long ago that it does no good to worry about these things," the woman was saying now. She'd been chattering away for several minutes, but DJ hadn't been listening too well.

"What's that?" asked DJ.

"I was just saying that worrying doesn't help anything, dear."

"Oh."

"And I can tell by your expression that you're getting worried."

"I was just wondering if going to Las Vegas for Christmas was a good idea after all."

"Then why are you going, dear?"

DJ shrugged. "It sounded like fun."

The woman shook her head. "I hope you will be careful. Las Vegas can be a very dangerous place. A pretty young girl like you could get into all kinds of trouble there."

"Really?"

"Most certainly. I've heard all sorts of stories. Especially if you're not staying at a reputable place."

"We're staying at a hotel called Mandalay Bay, and we'll be there until New Year's—"

The woman's brows lifted now. "Goodness, that's a very nice hotel—and rather expensive too, especially for that long of a time. I'm surprised young people can afford such things. It's not like it was when I was a college coed."

So DJ opened up and told the woman about Taylor and her mother and the generous invitation, and how she was going primarily because it seemed that Taylor was lonely. She left out the part about going to make sure that Taylor didn't get into trouble.

"Well, that's very thoughtful of you, dear. I'm sure it will be worth whatever little inconveniences you may experience while traveling." The woman patted her hand. "Now, that we know each other better, I think we should introduce ourselves. My name is Clara Snider."

"I'm DJ Lane. It's nice to meet you Mrs. Snider."

"Oh, you can call me Clara." She chuckled. "Who knows … we may know each other quite well if our flight continues to be delayed."

Unfortunately, one delay seemed to turn into another until it was nearly eight at night and all flights were cancelled.

"Is there any point in trying to get a hotel?" DJ asked the agent at the gate.

"No. For one thing, I doubt you'd get one." She handed DJ a plastic-encased blanket and pillow from the plane. "Besides that, there's a chance this flight will get out around six a.m. if the storm lets up like they're predicting. In that case, you'd need to be back here before four and, if you think about it, it's hardly worth it."

"Can I have another pillow and blanket for my friend?" DJ glanced over to where Clara was snoozing in her seat.

"Here you go." The agent lowered her voice. "And here's a tip. If you didn't bring any food, you might want to go get something before it's too late."

"Too late?"

"Meaning before everyone figures out that they're spending the night here."

"Right."

DJ hurried back to Clara, piled the blankets and pillows on the chair where she had left her book and jacket, and then headed out to forage for food. As it turned out, the gate agent was right. The air terminal was packed with thousands of travelers who'd been stuck in O'Hare all day. Every restaurant had long, crowded lines, and signs were posted announcing which foods were already starting to run out. According to the news, the roads surrounding Chicago were a mess as well, and the prediction was that delivery trucks would be delayed as a result. But somehow DJ managed to gather an assortment of fresh fruit, crackers, nuts, and candy bars, as well as several bottles of water—enough, she figured, for both her and Clara. On her way back to her seat, she phoned Taylor with the latest news.

"No way!" cried Taylor. "You *have* to make it in tonight."

"It's not possible." DJ stuffed a water bottle into her backpack.

"Bummer!"

"Tell me about it."

"Did you get a hotel?"

DJ glanced around the packed terminal, where people were already setting up makeshift campsites and preparing for a long night. "Yeah, right. Earth to Taylor. It's a blizzard here, all flights are cancelled, it's holiday traffic, and the hotels are full."

"Ugh! That's too bad. Spending the night in O'Hare … sounds like a nightmare."

"Well, at least I've made a friend to keep me company."

"A guy? Is he hot? Maybe you can cuddle up with him and stay warm."

DJ laughed. "It's an old woman, Taylor."

"Oh. It figures. Call me when you know you're coming in. I'll send out a limo."

"Like six in the morning?"

"Maybe not. Just call the hotel. I'll arrange it so that it goes on our bill. Okay?"

DJ sighed. "Okay."

"And DJ," Taylor's voice softened a little. "Be careful, okay?"

"Thanks. Hopefully I'll see you sometime tomorrow."

DJ pressed her way back through the crowds of people until she reached the right gate, which was even more packed now than before.

"I foraged for us," said DJ as she held up her bulging backpack.

"Bless you, child," said Clara.

"I figured I better get some food before it was gone."

"Smart girl." Clara reached for her oversize handbag. "I brought a few things to munch on, but they're mostly gone." Now Clara set her rolling carry-on bag between them like a low table, arranging a napkin like a tablecloth as DJ unpacked the food. Then Clara bowed her head. "For what we are about to receive, make us truly thankful. Amen."

DJ grinned at her. "Cool."

Clara laughed. "Yes. Cool." Then she opened her handbag to produce a small jar of peanut butter and some mozzarella string cheese.

"That will be perfect with the crackers," said DJ.

"It's like the loaves and fishes," Clara declared. "God always provides."

After they finished their meal, Clara produced a deck of cards. "Do you play gin rummy?"

DJ admitted she didn't know how, and Clara offered to teach her. By midnight, DJ had the game down, but she could tell Clara was worn out. "Would you like to try to find a place to lie down?" asked DJ, suddenly concerned with the old woman's welfare.

"I hate to give up our seats." Clara glanced around the crowded area. "It's possible we might not find a better spot."

"Why don't you stay here while I look around," suggested DJ. But when DJ walked through the terminal, she could see it was futile. The place was packed. Finally, back at her own gate, she saw the weary-looking ticket agent and decided to approach her.

"I'm worried about my friend over there," said DJ. "She's pretty old to be sitting up all night. Do you know anywhere she could lie down?"

The agent looked behind the counter. "I guess you could both have this area back here. I'm about to leave anyway."

"Thanks!" DJ looked at the small space which suddenly seemed like a plush, private room. "I'll be right back."

"I found something," said DJ, grabbing up their things. "Up there."

Soon DJ had managed to make a "mattress" of sorts from the clothing in their carry-on bags and their coats. "It's not the Ritz," she admitted.

"It's lovely," said Clara. "And you are an angel."

After they were both settled down, Clara sighed. "It reminds me of the first Christmas. Mary and Joseph . . . in Bethlehem . . . no room at the inn . . . but God took care of them . . . they made do . . . and then the Savior was born."

DJ considered this. But before she could respond, she heard the quiet sounds of Clara's snores. And that's when it hit DJ — if she hadn't connected with Clara today, if she'd been by herself in this crazy, crowded terminal — stuck here for the night — she would've been feeling vulnerable and scared right now. As it was, she felt safe and protected. It's as if God sent Clara to be her angel. And then DJ went to sleep too.

10

LOST in Las Vegas

"I'D LIKE YOU TO meet my latest guardian angel." Clara politely introduced DJ to her son. The three of them were standing amidst the crowd clamoring around the baggage carousel, watching for their bags to pop out.

He shook DJ's hand. "Thanks for helping my mom in Chicago."

DJ laughed. "I thought she was the one who helped me."

Soon they had gathered their bags and were making their way to the ground transportation area. "You sure you don't need a ride?" Clara's son asked DJ for the second time.

"I'm supposed to be picked up," DJ assured them. She tried not to look nervous as she glanced around the busy area.

"Well, you take care now." Then Clara kissed DJ on the cheek and departed with her son. Suddenly DJ felt very much alone—alone in a big crowd. She walked around, watching as people connected with loved ones, grabbed taxis or shuttles, all hurrying on their way. She seemed to be the only one who had no idea of what to do or where to go. And she was getting more and more frustrated. Even though it wasn't yet eight a.m., she was about to call Taylor when she suddenly noticed a man dressed in a neat black uniform holding up a sign that said DJ Lane. In relief, she waved at him, hurrying down the sidewalk toward him. "That's me!" she exclaimed.

"DJ Lane?" He gave her a scrutinizing look.

"Yes." She glanced down at her rumpled clothes, then quickly explained how she'd spent last night sleeping on the floor of an air terminal.

"Eva Perez sent me to get you." He gathered her bags and nodded to the black stretch Hummer limo that was waiting right next to him. DJ had to laugh as she remembered her last ride in a rig like this. Okay, maybe that Hummer had been white, but this one smelled a whole lot better. And this one she had all to herself.

"Wow," said DJ as he helped her into the back. "I feel like a rock star."

He just nodded politely, then closed the door.

She leaned back into the comfortable leather seat and sighed. This was quite a departure from sleeping on the floor of an airport. She peered out the window, trying to take in the glittering billboards and tall buildings. It wasn't long until they were at the hotel. The driver unloaded her bags and handed them off to another guy in a uniform who led her to a registration desk, informing the clerk that she was "a guest of Ms. Perez."

"Yes, I just need to see your ID and have you sign here," the woman told her. Then she was given a key and a room number, and the next thing she knew she was walking into what looked like a very expensive home. Their suite had a spacious living area that looked out over a large pool, a full-size kitchen and dining area, and a hallway with several closed doors. The bellboy set her bags inside and, without even waiting for a tip, quickly made himself scarce. The suite was quiet. Since it was only a little past nine, DJ guessed that her hosts were still sleeping. She made herself comfortable on the large sectional and fell quickly to sleep as well.

"You're finally here!" exclaimed Taylor. DJ sat up and attempted to get her bearings. For a moment she thought she was back home with Taylor in their shared room. But then she noticed the plush surroundings and remembered Vegas.

"Yes, finally." DJ yawned and stretched. "Pretty nice digs you got here."

"It's the best they have," said Taylor. "Penthouse suite ... although we still have to share a room. But at least it has two queen beds."

"What time is it?"

"A little past one." Taylor tied the belt of her short black satin robe and glanced toward the kitchen. "You hungry?"

"Actually, I'm ravenous."

"I was thinking of heading down to the pool. I could call in an order and have it delivered to our cabana."

"Our cabana?"

"Yes, we have the use of a cabana while we're here. Number 14."

"A cabana, like, on a beach?"

"Actually, there is a beach here."

"A beach? I thought we were in Las Vegas. Isn't that sort of landlocked?"

"The hotel has a pool with waves and sand like a beach. It's not bad, unless there are too many kiddies playing." Taylor pointed out the big window. "See, it's down there, past the other pools—that big one."

DJ nodded. "Interesting."

"Why don't you meet me down there after you clean up and unpack your stuff?"

"A shower does sound good, and it shouldn't take too long to unpack since I'm traveling pretty light."

"Didn't you borrow some of my clothes like I told you to do?"

DJ frowned. "I didn't really want to go through your things, Taylor. Not when you weren't there. It would feel weird."

Taylor laughed. "Hey, I would go through your things if I wanted."

"I'm sure you would."

"Anyway, by the time you get down there, I should have things pretty much set for lunch."

"In cabana 14?"

"That's right. I'll just order some salads and sandwiches—enough so that we can have guests if we like."

"Guests?" DJ frowned as she tried to imagine people crowding into a tiny tent. "In our cabana? How big is it anyway?"

Taylor just laughed. "Oh, DJ, you have so much to learn."

"And I'm sure you're just the person to teach me."

"Absolutely."

"And please tell me that you don't plan on wearing one of those ugly team suits to the pool."

"Why not?"

"DJ!"

"Hey, I had to pack in a hurry. It's not like you gave me much notice."

"Lucky for you, I did a little shopping in Phoenix. I'll put out some things for you to use while you're here. My *old* stuff—since I'll be wearing the new things."

DJ thanked her halfheartedly, then went into the bathroom. She knew that sometimes she just needed to bite her tongue with Taylor—otherwise they'd end up in some stupid fight that no one would win. Or maybe it was like that old saying, "pick your battles." Whatever the case, DJ was determined to do her best to get along with her prickly roommate.

She looked around the spacious bathroom—at least twice the size of the one they shared at home. Everything was elegant, modern, and luxurious. She quickly stripped down and got into the shower, trying to remember the last time a shower felt so good. Maybe it was after she'd gotten her cast off. But she knew this was a close second. She soaped up with some fantastic-smelling shower gel, feeling all the grit and grime of the air terminal washing down the drain. By the time she emerged from the bathroom wrapped in a thick cotton bathrobe, Taylor was gone.

But there on the bed that was still neatly made—presumably DJ's—was a small pile of summerlike clothes, including not just one, but two bikinis. DJ picked the more modest of the two. Then she put a white T-shirt and khaki shorts on over the suit and slipped into her favorite pair of leather flip-flops. Okay, she was not as sophisticated-looking as Taylor would like, but she was who she was. Then DJ dug out her sunglasses and sunscreen and a few other pool things. By the time she was ready to go down, it was getting close to two.

"Hello there," said a woman's smooth voice as DJ came into the living area. She turned to see Eva Perez in a silky, pale pink robe, her hair wrapped in a white bath towel like a turban. She was just sitting down to a tray of room-service food.

"Oh, hello, Ms. Perez." DJ smiled nervously, suddenly feeling like an intruder. "This is a beautiful hotel."

"Yes . . . it's nice. How was your trip, Desiree?"

"Much better now that I'm here, but you don't have to call me Desiree. I mostly go by DJ . . . except by my grandmother . . . she's kind of formal."

"All right, *DJ*. And in that case, please, don't call me Ms. Perez. My friends call me Eva." She poured coffee, then looked up. "Have you eaten?"

"No, I'm meeting Taylor for lunch."

"That's good, but feel free to call room service anytime you like. Or if you're anywhere in the hotel, just charge your expenses to the room."

"Thanks. And thank you for inviting me to come down. This seems like a really great place."

"It's a pleasure to have you with us."

"I was sort of surprised that my grandmother agreed to let me go."

"Yes, well, I suppose I may have twisted her arm."

DJ was surprised. "Really?"

"Oh, not too much. I actually think she was pleased that Taylor invited you. Your grandmother seems quite impressed with my daughter." She laughed lightly. "She has such high hopes for her as a professional model. I just hope Taylor doesn't disappoint her."

"I don't see how. So far, Taylor seems to have what it takes for modeling." But even as DJ said this, she knew there was more than one way that Taylor could disappoint Grandmother.

"Taylor has been lonely and at loose ends. I think she missed you."

DJ tried not to laugh. "Well, Taylor might not believe me, but I really missed her too."

Eva nodded with a look of understanding as she picked up a croissant and studied it. "I know that my daughter can be . . . well, difficult."

DJ didn't know what to say now.

"But Taylor has been through some pretty hard things. And she's been forced into a grown-up world . . . and her father and

I ... well, we weren't the best parents. I'm afraid we're a bit dysfunctional."

"I can relate to dysfunctional." But DJ would never use her messed-up family as an excuse to mess up her life. That was just plain dumb—kind of a double whammy.

"I realize that Taylor can be a headstrong young woman ... and although she's very intelligent, she doesn't always use the best common sense. I'm sure you've picked up on that by now."

DJ nodded slowly. She had to agree with her there.

"But it is reassuring to know that she has a good friend like you, DJ. You have no idea how much I appreciate that."

"Well ... thank you."

"Now, I know you have better things to do than listen to me going on and on." She waved her hand as if to dismiss DJ. "But just know this ... I am very, very grateful to have you here with us, DJ. And I want you to have a good time."

"Thanks."

"Thank *you*."

DJ felt mixed emotions as she rode the elevator down to the "beach level." For one thing, she was touched by Eva's trust in her. But it also added some pressure. Did Eva, like Grandmother, expect DJ to keep Taylor out of trouble? To be her round-the-clock babysitter? Because, if that was the case, they were probably all heading for a disappointment. As she walked through the pool grounds, gazing up at gently swaying palm trees and feeling the soft warm breeze against her skin, DJ felt like she had landed in paradise. Oh, she knew that Las Vegas had been dubbed Sin City, but so far she had seen nothing to make her think it deserved the name. This place was absolutely beautiful. Far better than being stuck in wet, cold Connecticut. She eventually found her way to the right pool and cabana 14, which turned out to be a tented room complete with a mini kitchen, chairs, lounges, and a flat-screen TV. Who knew?

"Hey, you found it," said Taylor as she popped open what appeared to be a beer. Why should this surprise DJ? And yet it did.

"You're not worried about getting in trouble for underage drinking?"

Taylor just laughed. "Oh, DJ, you should know me better than that by now." She studied the blue metal container in her hand. It was shaped like a beer bottle. "But if it's any consolation, I'll try to keep the drinking to a minimum, okay?"

DJ didn't say anything, just frowned.

"Come on, that should make you happy."

"It'd make me happier if you didn't drink at all, Taylor."

Taylor rolled her eyes as she took a long sip. Then she dropped the can into the trash receptacle. It made such a solid *clunk*, that DJ thought that maybe it was still mostly full. That was something.

"The food should be here soon," Taylor informed her as she took out a cigarette and lit it. "Maybe that will improve your disposition."

"Meaning I'm a grouch?"

Taylor shrugged. "Just a buzz-kill mainly."

"So what else is new?"

Taylor nodded toward the mini fridge now. "There are sodas in there for you."

"Thanks." DJ opened the fridge and removed a raspberry soda.

"Want to get me a ginger ale?" called out Taylor as she arranged herself on a lounge chair. "With ice too?"

DJ located plastic tumblers and filled them with ice and soda, then took them over to the lounge chairs. "Here you go." She sat down on the chair next to Taylor. "Look, I didn't come here to ruin your fun. But you know who I am, right? And you knew who I was before you asked me to come down here. If that's a problem, why not just lay your cards on the table right now? Maybe I can get my flight changed and go home."

"No, I don't want you to go home. I just want you to lighten up a little, okay?" Taylor lowered her oversized sunglasses and looked over them with an intense expression. "Can't we just have some fun and a few laughs and call it good?"

"I guess so."

Taylor held up her soda glass in a hesitant toast. "Viva Las Vegas then?"

"Well, here's to knocking the sin part out of Sin City."

"And still have fun?" queried Taylor.

"More fun."

Taylor seemed to consider this as she sipped her soda. "Hey, check out that guy in the blue boardshorts."

DJ peered across the pool to see a tall Latino guy walking their direction. "Not bad."

"His name is Tony, and he has a friend named Arden. Want to invite them to lunch?"

"What about Seth?" asked DJ.

"What about him?"

"I thought you were still going with him."

"Duh … I am. But we're not married. Not even engaged, for that matter."

"I know, but how would he feel about you picking up another guy in Vegas?"

Taylor laughed loudly. "I'm not picking up anyone. I just want to have some fun, and it doesn't hurt to have a guy or two around to do it." She nudged DJ now. "See that blond guy in the green boardshorts? That's Arden."

"So?"

"So, do you think he's hot?"

"I guess … but if you're trying to get me a date, I'm not interested, okay?"

"Because you're being true to Conner?"

"Maybe."

"Do you honestly think that Conner is oblivious to the pretty little ski bunnies that are flirting with him up in Montana?"

"That's not really the point." Still, this hadn't really occurred to DJ. Not that she'd use it as an excuse for anything now. But she hoped that her relationship with Conner meant as much to him as it did to her.

"Look, DJ, I'm not asking you to have this guy's baby. I'm just saying, what's wrong with hanging with a couple of nice guys?"

DJ shrugged. "I don't know."

"If nothing else, it's a good way to keep the jerks at bay."

DJ considered this. Maybe Taylor was on to something. "I guess it doesn't hurt to get to know them."

"I already know them."

"And?"

"And they're just a couple of regular guys. Not that different from Conner and Seth, just a little older. In fact, you should be impressed to learn that they go to Stanford." Now Taylor was waving, and it was clear that the Stanford dudes were heading their way.

"Aren't you a little overdressed for the pool?" Taylor asked as she adjusted a strap on her bikini top.

"I'm comfortable."

"Whatever." Taylor smiled up at the guys, then quickly introduced them to DJ. "We're roommates," she explained. "And I begged her to come out here and keep me company."

"That's some nice company," said Arden. DJ wasn't sure if he was talking about Taylor or her, although his eyes seemed to be on her. And now she was starting to feel nervous.

"Help yourself to drinks," said Taylor. "You know where everything is."

"Thanks," said Tony as he popped open a beer. "You're like the hostess with the mostest."

Arden laughed. "And you're like the corndog of the corniest, Tony."

"At last—here comes the food," announced Taylor. She nodded to where a couple of cabana boys were carrying some large trays toward the cabana.

"Let the party begin!" shouted Tony.

DJ wasn't so sure.

"YOU'RE WHERE?" ASKED RHIANNON.

"Vegas," said DJ calmly. She was still down at the pool, where Taylor was partying with her poolside buddies. And, true to her word, Taylor wasn't really drinking much. But her friends were. DJ had called Rhiannon for some moral support.

"With Taylor?" Rhiannon's voice sounded incredulous.

"Yes." DJ quickly explained how and why she'd come.

"Wow . . . that's so weird. Christmas in Vegas."

"And now I'm starting to question the whole thing. I mean it seemed like God opened the door. But suddenly I'm not so sure."

"Maybe God just wants you to be a light in a dark place."

"Vegas is actually a pretty bright place." DJ squinted up at the clear blue sky. "I mean there are lights and things all over."

"I'm not talking about physical light and dark."

"I know . . . but it is a little ironic if you think about it."

"Just think of it as darkness masquerading as light," said Rhiannon. "Kind of like Satan."

"Huh?"

"Well, Satan was an angel of light."

"Seriously?"

"That's what it says in the Bible, but I think I'm digressing. The point is that you need to be a light, DJ."

"How?"

"By letting Jesus shine through you."

"How?" she asked again.

"By making sure that you're connected to him."

"That's all?"

"Yeah. Kind of like a lightbulb. It just needs to be screwed in tightly to the source of electricity, and, voila, it lights up."

"If the switch is on."

"So make sure the switch is on."

DJ glanced over to where Taylor was laughing with one arm slung casually around Tony's tanned shoulders. This wasn't going to be easy. "How are things going for you, Rhiannon? How is it with your mom?"

"It's okay. It helps being here at Aunt Ruby's. She's pretty groovy for an old lady. And you should see her closet! It's full of all these great clothes from the forties and fifties — we're talking major retro. Plus she's a strong Christian, and she's been having some good talks with my mom."

"Cool."

"Yeah. So far it is."

"Well, I'm still praying for you and your mom."

"And now I'll be praying for you and Taylor."

"Thanks."

"I should probably go help Aunt Ruby with dinner."

"And I should probably go light up Las Vegas."

Rhiannon laughed. "Hang in there, DJ."

"You too."

But DJ did feel better when she closed her phone. As she walked back over to the cabana, she silently prayed, asking God to light her up for others to see.

"Hey, there you are," said Taylor. "Who was on the phone?"

"Rhiannon."

"Everything okay with her?" Taylor actually seemed interested.

"Yeah. Groovy."

Tony laughed. "You sound like my mom. Only she says groovy bassaroovy, whatever that means."

"Hey, DJ, give me a hand over here," said Taylor as she went over by the kitchenette.

DJ joined her and helped herself to another sandwich. "With what?"

"Just pretend to help me," said Taylor quietly. "And listen."

So DJ pretended to busy herself with straightening the veggie platter.

"Look, I've told these guys some things, you know, and I just want you to play along. Okay?"

"Play along how?"

"Just follow my lead."

DJ shrugged and popped a cucumber into her mouth.

Soon Taylor was introducing her to a few others who had joined the little party—a couple of college girls from LA and some guys from here and there. DJ wasn't really keeping very close track of the names and places. But she smiled and imagined that she was being a light.

"So I hear you and Taylor are models," said the dark-haired girl. DJ thought her name was Katie. "From New York?"

"We actually live in Connecticut," DJ corrected her. "And we're not—"

"Have you ever heard of Katherine Carter?" asked Taylor quickly. "She was a really famous model back in the fifties and sixties, and then she ran *Couture* up until a few years ago."

"Oh, yeah," said Katie. "I know who you mean. She was like some mega-fashion diva, right?"

"And she's still quite respected in the fashion world. Anyway we actually live with her in Connecticut. And she manages us."

DJ kind of laughed. "Or mismanages us, as the case may be."

"So what kind of modeling do you do?" asked the blonde girl.

"So far just runway," said Taylor. "But I think Mrs. Carter is looking into some print possibilities too."

"Like fashion magazines?" asked Katie.

Taylor tossed a thick strand of dark curls over her shoulder and nodded with a bored expression. "And catalogs."

DJ was trying to figure out something to say that would set these girls straight, but to be fair, Taylor hadn't actually lied ... just misled.

"And you're really going to be in Fashion Week?" asked the blonde girl. She seemed to be directing this to DJ, almost as if she wasn't buying this. "In New York City?"

"Yes. We're doing a show for a new designer."

"Who?" demanded Katie.

"You probably haven't heard of him." Taylor glanced at DJ, and DJ knew that Taylor couldn't remember his name.

"Dylan Marceau," said DJ.

"That sounds kind of familiar," said the blonde. "I'll have to google him."

Taylor nodded. "Yes, you'd probably like his designs. They're not terribly sophisticated ... more of a practical sort of fashion."

DJ smirked at Taylor. "He designs clothes you can actually wear, not just strut around in."

"Speaking of strutting," said Katie. "Can you guys show us how to do the walk—you know the one they do on the runway."

DJ laughed. "Not me. If you want to see really good strutting, have Taylor show you."

Soon they were all urging Taylor to strut her stuff, but Taylor was brushing them off.

"Come on," said Tony. "Show us how it's done, Taylor."

Now Taylor just shrugged. "Fine. Watch and learn." And, just like that, she went over to an open area and executed a perfect catwalk up and down the deck next to the pool. Even the music seemed to cooperate with her as she held her head high and placed one foot in front of the next, strutting confidently past sunbathers who couldn't help but look up and watch. And when she finished, everyone—including the slightly stunned sunbathers—applauded with enthusiasm.

"Wow," said Tony when Taylor rejoined them at the cabana. "That was hot."

"You really are good," admitted Katie with surprise.

"Can you teach us?" asked the blonde.

"I could," said Taylor. "But I'm not going to."

Tony laughed. "Give the girls a break. They're on vacation."

"That's right," agreed Arden. "It's not like this is some reality make-me-a-model TV show."

"Thank goodness for that," said DJ.

The girls still peppered DJ and Taylor with modeling questions until DJ was getting a little fed up. So she decided to change the subject. "So, do you know who Taylor's mother is?"

Taylor tossed DJ a slightly exasperated look, but it was too late.

"Someone famous?" asked Arden with curiosity.

"Anyone heard of Eva Perez?" DJ glanced around the group.

Katie nodded. "Oh, yeah, she's performing here."

"Is that your mom?" asked Arden, clearly impressed.

Taylor nodded, then went over to the mini fridge and pulled out a beer. DJ got the distinct feeling that Bud was for her. She probably should've kept her mouth shut. But, in a way, Taylor had started it with the modeling bit.

"Can you get us a deal on tickets?" asked Tony hopefully.

Taylor shrugged. "You really want to hear her?"

"Oh, yeah. My parents are big fans of Eva Perez. It'd be great to tell them that I saw her in person." He smiled at Taylor. "And that I actually hung with her daughter, the famous New York fashion model."

Arden nodded. "Yeah, I can't wait to tell the guys back at school. They'll be sorry they didn't come to Vegas with us."

"I can probably get some tickets," said Taylor casually.

"I'd like to hear her too," admitted DJ. "I've been a fan for a while."

"It figures." Taylor rolled her eyes and took a long sip.

DJ could take a hint. Taylor wasn't pleased that DJ had switched the limelight from them to her mother. Well, whatever. "I'm going to take a swim," DJ announced to no one in particular.

"Need any company?" asked Arden.

DJ made a nonchalant face at him. "Well, if you think you can keep up."

Arden laughed like he thought she was joking.

Of course, once he got into the pool and realized that DJ meant it, and that she was swimming laps—fast laps—he wasn't laughing anymore. After awhile, he gave up completely, which suited her just fine. The workout felt good, and the water was cool and refreshing after the stuffy cabana. She soon lost count of how many laps she'd swum, but by the time she got out of the pool, Taylor's cabana party seemed to be in full swing.

"You didn't tell us that you were an Olympic swimmer," commented Arden, as DJ returned with a towel wrapped around her like a sari.

"Models, singers, swimmers ..." Katie held up her hands in a hopeless gesture. "You girls just seem to have it *all* going on." But DJ could tell that Katie was still skeptical and maybe more than a little jealous. Not that it was DJ's problem. This was Taylor's gig, not hers.

DJ grabbed another sandwich and a soda and made herself comfortable in a lounge chair. Her plan was to feign a nap while she caught some rays and avoided having to engage with the partiers. But it wasn't long before she was really getting sleepy. So she turned over to sun her back and quickly fell asleep.

The next thing she knew something cold was dripping down her back. Thinking someone had spilled something, she jumped up to see Arden standing over her with a bottle of sunscreen in hand. "Taylor told me to come give you a hand," he said nervously. "So you don't get burned."

"Oh." DJ frowned at him then lay back down. "Thanks."

"Don't let this December sun fool you," he said as he rubbed the lotion onto her shoulders. "It burns just the same as in July."

"Uh-huh," she muttered, wishing he'd hurry it up. He seemed to be enjoying the process a little too much.

"So what do you think of Vegas?" he asked as he rubbed lotion onto her back.

"I don't really know. I just got here this morning." Maybe she could drop him a hint now. "But after being stranded at O'Hare overnight, I'd have to admit that this is an improvement."

"You spent the night at the airport?"

"Yeah, and I'm exhausted. So don't mind me if I doze off."

"Sure ... don't let me disturb you." Now she heard the lid click back onto the lotion bottle, and he returned to the partiers. She closed her eyes and sighed in relief. This was going to be a long week.

DJ woke up to the sound of her cell phone ringing. She fumbled through her bag and found it in time to discover it was Casey. "Hey, Casey!" said DJ happily. "What's up?"

"Is it true?" demanded Casey.

"What?"

"Are you really in Vegas with Taylor?"

"Where'd you hear that?"

"Rhiannon. I called her a little while ago, and she told me the whole thing, but I just can't believe it. Is it true?"

"Yeah."

"Have you lost your mind?"

"It's possible."

"So where are you right now? What are you doing? What's Taylor doing? Tell me everything."

"There's not much to tell," admitted DJ. "I mean, we're at the pool. Taylor has a cabana for us to use for the week. It's like a little house, with a mini kitchen and furnishings and even a flat-screen TV."

"Wow! That sounds cool."

DJ sat up now. "Yeah, it is kind of cool." Next she described their luxurious suite.

"Now I'm starting to get seriously jealous."

DJ laughed, then lowered her voice. "Don't forget, I'm with Taylor."

"Kind of like paying your dues."

"I guess."

"Even so, I wouldn't mind being in your shoes."

"I'm not wearing shoes."

"Hey, maybe I could borrow the car and drive over."

"How far is your parent's place from Vegas?"

"Probably five hundred miles, give or take."

"That's a pretty long drive."

"Yeah, my parents would probably say forget it."

DJ didn't want to mention that Casey's parents would probably say to forget it for other reasons too — primarily being that this was Las Vegas. "How are your parents doing?" DJ decided to change the subject.

"Okay, I guess."

"Bet they were glad to see you."

"Meaning that they were relieved to see that I lost the Mohawk and piercings?"

"Yeah, whatever."

"They think your grandmother is a miracle worker."

"Did you set them straight?"

"Are you kidding? If I did that, they probably wouldn't let me go back."

Then DJ told Casey about Fashion Week.

"Well, it's a small price to pay," said Casey. "I mean to get back with my friends."

DJ smiled. It was nice to hear that from Casey — to hear that she considered the Carter House girls her friends. Who would've thought? They wrapped up their conversation. As DJ hung up, she heard Taylor calling out to her.

"Looks like we're going to Mama Mia tonight," announced Taylor.

"The musical?" asked DJ, confused.

Taylor laughed. "No, I mean we're going to hear my mom in concert. Mama mia, get it?"

"And Taylor invited Arden and me to tag along too," said Tony.

"Hope you don't mind," said Arden apologetically.

"And if you do," said Katie eagerly, "I'd be happy to take your place."

"I could only get four tickets," Taylor told DJ, with a look that suggested perhaps she'd only wanted four tickets. "I think it's sold out, but, hey, if you're not interested—"

"No," said DJ quickly. "Count me in."

"Cool," said Arden, as if this somehow made this an official double date.

DJ forced a smile and figured she could set him straight later. But maybe she'd have to set Taylor straight first. Like that was possible.

"THIS Dress," Taylor Insisted as she thrust a short, black sequined number at DJ. They were back in the room now, getting ready for the concert.

DJ frowned at the skimpy cocktail dress. "I think it's too old for me."

"No, it's not. Just try it on, okay?"

"I don't have shoes to—"

"I have shoes. Come on. Just try it. We're going to a concert in Vegas, DJ. It's okay to dress up and have fun."

DJ reluctantly took the dress off the hanger and carefully unzipped it. "This is a Vera Wang. It must've cost a fortune—"

"Don't freak, DJ. It was my mom's. She probably got it for free—or nearly. Anyway, she doesn't like it."

"And she doesn't mind if I wear it?"

"No, of course not. I'd wear it myself, except that it's too tight," Taylor thrust out her well-endowed chest, "and my girls don't like feeling restrained."

DJ laughed, then slipped on the dress. Although it was pretty short, she had to admit that it was somewhat conservative in the neckline. Kind of a Jackie O look, really. "Not bad," she said as she checked it out in the mirror.

"It's perfect for you." Taylor nodded. "And I have the perfect shoes to go with it."

"Wow," said DJ when she saw Taylor adjusting a strap of her ruby-red satin dress. "You look really hot."

Taylor held her head high. "I certainly hope so." She joined DJ in front of the mirror. "The question is do I look hotter than you?" Now she frowned as if unsure.

"Of course, you do," said DJ quickly. "You always do."

"I don't know ..." Taylor frowned. "Blondes in black ... I should've thought this one through a little better."

"It's not like we're competing. And what about brunettes in red? Shouldn't there be a rule against it?"

Taylor smiled smugly. "I do look hot, don't I?"

DJ nodded.

"And we haven't even done makeup or accessories yet."

Taylor pulled open a couple of bathroom drawers, and the two girls continued to primp. DJ decided to keep her accessories simple, which Taylor agreed was the right thing. "Sophisticated and understated," she told DJ. "Should we put your hair up, to help hide those damaged ends?"

DJ gave her long blonde hair a shake. "I think it's fine down."

"Fine, if you like going around with chlorine-zapped hair."

"Whatever. Put it up if you want. But you know that I'm hopeless when it comes to doing hair."

"We need Rhiannon here." Taylor grabbed a brush and attacked DJ's hair, brushing and brushing and finally twisting it into a fairly nice-looking style. "How's that?"

"Not bad."

Now Taylor swept her dark curls up into a tumbled sort of do with tendrils hanging down here and there. Next she helped DJ with her makeup. "Looks like you got a little too much sun," she observed as she applied some eye shadow. DJ still couldn't get the hang of eye shadow.

"Do I look burnt?" asked DJ.

"A little pink. But it'll probably tan out."

DJ looked at Taylor's perfect bronze skin. "I wish I had your coloring."

Taylor laughed. "If I had a dollar for every time I heard that line."

"It's not a line. Your skin is gorgeous, and you know it."

Taylor shrugged. "It's not everyone's cup of tea."

"Viva la difference."

Taylor smiled into the mirror now. "We actually make a good pair—complementary coloring, you know."

DJ struck a pose. "Yes, we are rather striking, aren't we?"

"We'll knock 'em dead."

"By the way," said DJ. "I don't want Arden thinking that this is a date. He doesn't, does he?"

"Who knows what he thinks?"

"Well, it's not a date," said DJ firmly.

"What difference does it make?"

"I just don't want him to think that I'm into him, because I'm not."

"You don't think he's good-looking?"

"Of course, he's good-looking. But there's Conner. Remember?"

Taylor chuckled. "And remember, what happens in Vegas stays in Vegas."

"Nothing like that is going to happen to me."

"You never know." Taylor gave herself a final squirt of a perfume that looked expensive and smelled exotic.

The plan was to meet the guys downstairs, and since Eva was performing in the hotel, they could simply walk. Naturally, Taylor paired off with Tony, which left DJ and Arden together—like a couple.

"You look great," said Arden as they walked behind Taylor and Tony.

"Thanks."

"The guys back at our frat aren't going to believe this."

"Believe what?" asked DJ.

"That we took out the two hottest babes in Vegas. Professional models."

DJ stopped walking now and turned to Arden. "That's not exactly how it is."

"Huh?"

"I mean, yes, we are modeling. But you need to understand—"

"DJ!" Taylor had turned around and was calling to her. "Come on, we need to get in there before they close the doors."

Arden linked his arm in DJ's and hurried her along to catch up.

"I'll explain later," she told him as she tried to keep up. Her leg, although healed, still hurt sometimes, and running in high heels was not helping one bit.

As it turned out, Taylor was right. They were about to close the doors, and the four of them made it just in time.

"We're down in front," said Taylor.

"Wow, great seats," said Arden as they slipped past others who were already seated. And then the lights went down and the music started. Suddenly, there was Eva in a perfectly round spotlight. She began to sing, and DJ wasn't sure if she'd ever heard anything more beautiful. Really, it was nothing short of amazing. And to think DJ was sharing a penthouse suite with that woman and her daughter.

"That was spectacular," gushed DJ when the foursome emerged from the theater. "Your mother is incredible, Taylor."

"So I've heard."

"She's amazing," said Arden. "I'm going to get some of her CDs."

"My parents are going to be so jealous," said Tony. "Thanks for inviting us, Taylor."

"And to show our thanks, we made dinner reservations," said Arden.

"You girls hungry?" asked Tony.

"I'm starving," said Taylor.

"Me too," admitted DJ. Okay, this still didn't make it a date, but no way was DJ going to say no to food tonight.

After they were seated in what appeared to be a very elegant, and probably expensive, restaurant, Arden turned to DJ. "You were about to tell me something on our way to the concert."

DJ glanced over to see Taylor giving her a narrowed-eye warning, and so DJ decided to play it safe. "What?" she said absently.

"Something you were about to say?"

DJ shrugged. "I don't recall. Maybe it wasn't important."

The waiter appeared and asked what they wanted to drink. Without blinking, Taylor ordered a cosmo. And the waiter didn't ask for ID. Then Tony and Arden both ordered pale ale. "And you, miss?" The waiter looked at DJ, probably guessing that she was underage. Although she didn't know why he hadn't carded the others.

"A Pelligrino, please." The only reason DJ knew about this brand of bottled water was because her grandmother wouldn't dream of drinking water straight from the tap. At least it sounded somewhat grown-up. Not that DJ cared or felt the need to impress anyone. Mostly she was aggravated—and hungry. After dinner, when she was alone with Taylor, she would have to establish some ground rules about drinking. Although, to be honest, DJ wasn't even sure what they would be. It wasn't as if she could force Taylor to knock it off. But at the same time, it seemed wrong to say nothing. Wouldn't that be like condoning it? Now she was curious about these two college dudes. It was entirely possible that they too were underage.

"So, how do you guys like Stanford?" she asked when there was a break in conversation. They gave her pretty generic answers, which almost made her wonder if they actually went to Stanford. Maybe, like Taylor, they were putting on a big act.

"What year are you?" she asked.

The guys exchanged quick glances, then Tony answered. "Seniors."

DJ nodded. "What's your major?"

Taylor laughed now. "What is this, DJ? The Spanish Inquisition?"

Tony laughed too. "Yeah, for a minute there I thought I was talking to my mom."

Arden just smiled. "No big deal. I'm a GES major."

"What's that?" asked DJ.

"A glorified rock hound," teased Tony.

"Geological and environmental sciences."

DJ nodded. "Impressive."

"He wants to save the planet," said Tony.

"Nothing wrong with that," said DJ.

"Okay, you guys," said Taylor as the drinks arrived. "Time to lighten up."

DJ felt slightly relieved to know that Arden seemed like a legitimate college student with a respectable major. But if he was a senior, he was at least five years older than she was, and that made her even more uncomfortable. She knew she wasn't really doing anything wrong, but how would she feel if Conner got wind of the fact that she was here right now? On the other hand, she remembered what Taylor had said about snow bunnies in Montana. Of course, that was silly. Conner was on a family ski trip. She was in Las Vegas—unsupervised and with Taylor! Very different situations indeed.

Now the waiter was taking their orders, and Taylor was going all out by ordering lobster. "You guys don't have to get the bill," she told Tony lightly. "We can go Dutch."

"Yes," said DJ eagerly. "Dutch is fine."

"No way," said Tony. "This is our treat. A thank you for the great concert."

So DJ went ahead and ordered a New York steak. Not to be spiteful, but because she was hungry.

"I like women who aren't afraid to eat," said Arden.

"I always thought models were more along the anorexic lines," admitted Tony.

Taylor laughed. "A lot of them are. Not me. I think all things are good in moderation."

DJ nearly choked on her water. Yeah, right. Moderation. That was a good one coming from Taylor.

Dinner turned out to be pretty good. Afterward, DJ made it clear that she was worn out. "Spending the night at O'Hare was pretty exhausting," she told them. "If you don't mind, I think I'll call it a night."

"Not me," said Taylor.

DJ frowned. Did this mean she needed to stick around and make sure that Taylor stayed out of trouble?

"It's only ten," pointed out Arden. "And this is Las Vegas, you know, the city that never sleeps."

"You can sleep in the morning, DJ," said Tony.

"Come on," urged Taylor. "Can't you just hang on until midnight?"

DJ considered this. "If I hang on until midnight, will you be ready to hang it up then?"

Taylor grinned. "Sure."

Okay, there was no way to know if Taylor was being sincere or not, but DJ decided to hold her to it. "Fine, but at midnight, we're done, okay?"

"Great," said Arden. "This is our last night in Vegas, and we need to do it up right."

"Yep," said Tony sadly. "Gotta be home for the holidays."

"I heard there's a great band at House of Blues tonight," suggested Arden.

"Sounds good to me," said Taylor.

But when they got to the club, DJ noticed that there was a security guy checking for ID. "Hey," she said to Taylor, "They're carding."

"So?" Taylor gave her a blank look.

"So . . . I don't have ID."

Now Taylor acted surprised, obviously an act for the guys. "Oh, crud, did you leave your wallet in the room, DJ?"

"I just—"

"Don't worry. I'm sure they'll let you in." Taylor smiled with confidence.

"They just card the ones who look too young," said Tony. "You'll be fine."

But as it turned out, they were all carded. Taylor, with her fake ID, had no problem waltzing on past. And apparently the guys passed muster as well, because now they were all on the other side of the red velvet cord. Only DJ remained, and suddenly she just wanted to bolt.

"I don't have ID," she admitted, ready to spill the beans ... and how sorry she was ... and how she'd never try this again. But then Taylor smoothly stepped back over, and with a perfectly manicured nail, she tapped the security dude on the chest, smiling directly into his beady eyes as if he was the best thing she'd ever seen in uniform. Okay, it wasn't really a uniform, just a stupid T-shirt with SECURITY across the front. Subtle.

"My friend left her ID upstairs in the penthouse," she cooed to the stocky man. "But, please tell me you're not going to make her go all the way up to the top floor to get it."

"She's with us," said Arden, like he was a rock star. "Can't you see she's obviously over twenty-one?"

"Yeah," added Tony. "She's a professional model, you know, doesn't she get some kind of respect for being a celebrity?" As if that had anything to do with breaking the law.

"Or should we take these girls to another club," added Arden, "where they'll be appreciated?"

The guard's brows drew together. DJ was ready to make a run for it—and she knew she could be fast, even in heels—but she imagined the guard grabbing her and holding her until the cops showed up. Then, with everyone watching, they'd put her into cuffs and haul her downtown and throw her into the cooler, or whatever they called it.

What was a nice Christian girl doing in a place like this anyway?

JUST AS SHE WAS READY TO BOLT, the security guy glanced to the left and to the right, then tilted his head ever so slightly toward the club.

"Okay, just this once. But next time you bring your ID, pretty lady." Then he winked at her as he unhooked the velvet cord that separated her from the others. And like an idiot, or maybe a lamb to the slaughter, she walked right on through. But her knees were shaking.

Taylor linked arms with DJ, grinning like she'd just won the first round. But DJ tossed Taylor a warning glance — she wanted her to know that she was ticked.

"You girls go grab that table that's just emptying out over there, and we'll get some drinks," said Tony. "Cosmo for Taylor and ... what do you want, DJ?"

"Iced tea," she said stiffly.

At the table, Taylor turned to DJ. "See, no big deal."

"It's a big deal to me," said DJ, glancing around nervously. "You and I need to talk later."

Taylor just shrugged. "Fine ... later."

DJ tried not to look as if she was seething as she silently sipped her iced tea. Fortunately, the music was loud enough to prohibit much conversation. And, to be fair, the blues band was pretty good. Still, DJ would be relieved when it was midnight. Not that she had any way to know, since she wasn't wearing a watch and she'd left her cell phone upstairs. But she knew it couldn't be too much longer. Hopefully, Taylor wouldn't back out of her promise by then. If Taylor did, DJ decided she would simply go back to the suite without her. And if Eva happened to inquire, DJ would honestly tell her that Taylor was downstairs sipping cosmos at a club for grown-ups. Then Taylor could deal with it later! Let her clean up her own messes!

The suite was quiet when DJ let herself in. It was no big surprise that Taylor opted to remain with the guys at the club. Arden had offered to escort DJ to the suite, but, irked at the whole situation, DJ briskly told them all good night and headed out. Of course, she soon realized that an escort might've been appropriate as she walked through the casino, getting more attention than she wanted. But finally she was safe in the suite. Judging by the room-service tray—a picked-over late dinner—and the black velvet pumps, DJ assumed that Eva was asleep in her room.

Consequently, DJ felt guilty. Was she letting Eva down by not doing a better job of babysitting her daughter? And yet, how could DJ possibly keep up, let alone keep track of someone like Taylor? Was it even possible? Once again, DJ questioned her sensibilities to get pulled into this scheme. What had she been thinking? As DJ got ready for bed, she realized how long she'd be stuck here. It was still several days until Christmas—not that she was looking forward to happy holidays in Vegas—but then she wasn't even booked to go home until several days after that. During this time, Taylor would probably want to go clubbing, pick up guys, get wasted ... cheerful things like that. What a totally skanky way to spend Christmas.

It was nearly one in the morning by the time DJ got into bed, and although she was exhausted, she was suddenly wide awake—and her mind was racing. What if something went wrong with Taylor tonight? What if Arden and Tony weren't who they said they were? What if they got her drunk and ... what if? What if? What if?

DJ got out of bed and went out into the living area. She stood in front of the expansive windows that looked out over the city lights and skyline. Clenching her fists in frustration, she looked out over the glittering city and felt so lonely that it hurt. Tears were burning in her eyes as she silently questioned God. *What is going on? Why am I here in Las Vegas for Christmas? Why do I feel so totally miserable? Did I make a big mistake? Was Grandmother a fool for letting me come? Am I an idiot for trying to play by the rules? Does it really make any difference? Why is life so confusing? Why?*

She wondered if there was any chance of getting her return flight changed, but figured it was probably hopeless to try to get a seat going anywhere this close to Christmas. Still, even the boring prospect of spending the holidays with her grandmother and the general seemed preferable to this form of torture.

"Help me, God," she prayed quietly. "I feel so lost and alone. I don't know why I'm here. I'm worried about Taylor. Please, help us both. Help me to make the best of this mess and help Taylor to be safe." She prayed for a while longer, and, to her amazement, she began to feel calmer inside. That reassuring sense of peace returned. She knew that somehow God was going to strengthen her—somehow she would get through this.

She was just heading back to bed when she heard the door clicking. With a pounding heart, imagining it was a break-in, DJ ducked behind a partial wall. But to her relief—and surprise—it was only Taylor.

"You decided to come home?" asked DJ quietly.

"Oh! You scared me." Taylor's eyes were wide as she tossed her bag onto the sectional. "Why aren't you asleep, Miss Party Pooper?"

"Because I was worried about you."

Taylor shook her head with an exasperated expression. "That's so ridiculous."

Now DJ stepped closer to Taylor, pointing a finger into her face. "No, it's not ridiculous. You're out drinking with guys you don't even know and—"

"Shhh!" Taylor nodded to the bedroom. "Keep it down, will ya?"

DJ glared at Taylor, then instead of saying anything, she headed to the bedroom and climbed back into bed. She wanted to lecture Taylor, remind her of stories of other young women—like Natalie Holloway, the poor girl who'd been abducted in Aruba—naïve young women who put themselves in harm's way, then paid the price. But what was the point? Taylor never listened. If she ever learned anything, it would probably be the hard way.

DJ could hear Taylor in the bathroom, and it sounded like she was turning on the shower. Well, at least she was safely home. And, as far DJ could see, she wasn't even drunk. And she hadn't really stayed out all that late. At least not long enough to get into serious trouble. Maybe that was something. Also, Tony and Arden said they'd be leaving tomorrow—driving back to

California. And before long it would be Christmas—surely Taylor would slow it down for Christmas.

What if Taylor didn't slow it down? What if she kept partying and clubbing? What if things totally spun out of control? What if she met new guys? What if she pushed the envelope even further? Suddenly DJ remembered Clara at the airport—it was like she could hear the old woman's voice, saying how it really never helped matters to worry. "It's better to pray, dear."

DJ began to pray again. She prayed until she felt herself finally beginning to relax. Somehow she would get through this. God would give her strength. And maybe there was a reason Taylor had needed her. She had come to help.

"Oh, by the way," said Taylor as she came out of the bathroom, rubbing lotion into her elbows. "I almost forgot to tell you ..."

"Huh?" DJ asked sleepily.

"I wasn't *alone* with those guys tonight."

"What?"

"You know how you thought I was out by myself with Arden and Tony? Remember?"

"Huh?" DJ suppressed a yawn.

"I wasn't alone."

"What do you mean?"

"I mean Eliza was with me."

DJ sat up in bed now, looking directly at Taylor. "What did you say?"

Taylor chuckled. "You should see your face, DJ. It looks like you saw a ghost."

"What did you just say?" repeated DJ, feeling like she was in a bad dream.

"Your face, you look like—"

"No! Before that."

"You mean that Eliza is here?"

"*Eliza Wilton?*"

"Who else?"

"How is that even possible?"

"Well, they have these great big super jets that fly really fast through the air, and you buy a ticket and you pack — "

"You know what I mean, Taylor. How is it possible that Eliza is here in Vegas? How?"

"I invited her."

DJ jumped out of bed, suddenly wide awake and staring at Taylor in shock. *"You invited Eliza here?"*

"Ooh, now you sound like my jealous lover."

DJ shook her head, trying to wrap her mind around this. It made absolutely no sense. "You're just jerking my chain around, aren't you? Trying to get back at me for ditching you with the guys tonight, right?"

"Not at all. It actually worked out rather well." She chuckled. "Tony and Arden were quite impressed. One beautiful babe walks out, and another walks in. Presto-change-o."

"Huh?" DJ slumped back onto the bed. She was too tired, and her brain was fuzzy. Suddenly she wondered which one of them had really been drinking tonight.

Taylor laughed. "I'm sorry, DJ. Let me cut to the chase."

"Please, do."

"That day you were stuck in O'Hare, I felt desperate. I thought maybe you weren't going to make it at all. And I was really lonely. And, in desperation, I called Eliza."

"*You* called Eliza? On purpose?"

"I just wanted to hear what she was up to. And, well, I'd had a few drinks ... and she told me she was bored in Kentucky, and in a moment of weakness I asked her if she wanted to come out here for a quick visit."

"How is that even possible? Isn't she on her way to France by now?"

"Not for two whole days. She arranged a practically direct flight out of Vegas and will arrive in Paris early on Christmas morning."

"You're serious?"

"Yeah ..." Taylor looked a little uneasy, like maybe she could even see how crazy this seemed. "I was a little surprised when she called to confirm this."

"And that was when?"

"Yesterday."

"But you didn't tell me?"

"I didn't want to upset you."

"What made you think I'd be upset?"

Taylor held out her hands. "Look at you."

DJ pressed her lips together. "I'm not upset. Just a little confused. Like when did you and Eliza become such great friends?"

"We're not."

"But you invited her—" DJ sat up suddenly. "Hey, if you invited her, where is she?"

"She has her own room, of course."

"Of course."

"And it's because of Eliza that we called it an early night. She was tired from flying."

"Oh, that's so reassuring."

"But we have big plans for tomorrow."

"Right."

"Arden was pretty into her." Taylor frowned. "You don't mind, do you? I mean, Arden really liked you, but you kind of gave him the slip."

"Of course, I don't mind." DJ wondered how much crazier this could get. This whole ordeal reminded her of Alice going

133

through the looking glass—everything was unreal. "What difference does it make anyway?" she asked. "I thought Arden and Tony were leaving tomorrow."

"Change of plans."

"It figures."

"They're driving home, so they can hang on a little longer if they want." Taylor chuckled. "And they want."

"Oh, hooray." DJ picked up her pillow and gave it a hard punch, and then another. Why had she come here? Why had she allowed Taylor to trick her ... again?

"We're going to have another cabana party tomorrow."

"Oh, I can hardly wait." DJ rolled her eyes.

"The weather is supposed to be really good."

"Whoop-tee-doo." DJ flopped back on her bed.

"Don't be mad, DJ."

"I'm not."

"It's just two days."

DJ sat up suddenly. "Hey, maybe I can get a flight out of here and—"

"Don't do that," said Taylor. "Eliza will be gone soon."

DJ didn't say anything.

"To be honest, I was pretty shocked when she called me to say she was really here," admitted Taylor. "I'd hoped that maybe it hadn't worked out. But her flight got in around seven. She checked in and took a shower and a nap, and the next thing I knew she was walking into ..."

But Taylor's words were falling on sleepy ears. DJ began to slip away, hoping that maybe she'd wake up and discover it had all been a bad dream. A silly nightmare. Because, really, Taylor wouldn't invite Eliza to Vegas. That was just insane.

14

LOST in Las Vegas

AS IT TURNED OUT, TAYLOR WAS INSANE. And the fact
that Eliza was here in Vegas seemed to be pretty good proof of
that. Not that DJ needed proof—she'd been fairly convinced
of Taylor's emotional instability before. As she pulled on her
sweats the next morning, she was hoping last night was a
dream or a hoax or even a hallucination. But when she stepped
out the door of their suite to see Eliza—dressed in pink and
white and smiling brightly with a Starbucks cup in hand—DJ
knew that Taylor was definitely out of her mind.

DJ frowned. "Excuse me," she said as she passed by her.

"Good morning, sunshine," called Eliza cheerfully. "I'll just
let myself in."

DJ didn't respond. Instead she hurried toward the elevators
and pulled her phone from her bag, turning it on to make sure
it was charged. Then as she rode down to the lobby, she fished
around in her bag until she found her e-ticket and searched for
the number of the airline. Of course, she was placed on hold,
so she got in line at Starbucks. While in line, DJ prayed—she
begged God to do a miracle and get her out of Vegas before

sunset. Wasn't he supposed to be the God of the impossible? She felt lost here. Lost and alone.

By the time she was halfway done with her mocha, an operator finally asked to assist her, and DJ explained her desperate need to change her departure date. Then the woman on the other end explained that it would be nearly impossible because of the holidays. "Please try," DJ urged her. "Anything sooner than what I have will be appreciated." This was followed by another long wait.

"The best I can do is the twenty-eighth, and that's an overnight flight, so you don't arrive until the twenty-ninth."

"That's the best?"

As it turned out, that was the best. DJ agreed to the change fee and booked it. It was only a few days sooner than her other ticket, but it was better than nothing. Or maybe she could take a train ... or a bus ... or hitchhike. Okay, maybe not hitchhike. But desperate times called for desperate measures.

DJ slowly walked through the quiet casino. There were a few glassy-eyed diehards still sitting in front of the slots, punching buttons again and again. DJ shook her head sadly — and that was supposed to be fun? She was heading back to the elevators when she realized that Eliza was probably sitting in the suite with Taylor right now, making big plans for her two days in Vegas.

DJ stopped and looked around, wishing for a place to hide, a way to escape Eliza and Taylor. Feeling totally discouraged, DJ sat down on a padded stool. She found herself in front of a slot machine — some goofy underwater thing with mermaids and starfish. It looked as if they were trying to appeal to children. Or maybe that's what Vegas was — a great big playground for grown-ups acting like children. Or children acting like grown-ups.

DJ noticed a security guard eyeing her. Was he trying to decide if she was old enough to gamble, or thinking of hitting on her? She wasn't sure, but to distract him, and perhaps in payment for her seat, she pulled out a dollar and slipped it into the machine. Really, what was the worst he could do? Have her arrested? Call her grandmother? Bring it! She punched the big red button and waited.

Suddenly the machine was making all kinds of noise. Lights were flashing and bells were ringing, and DJ actually jumped out of her seat. "What the—?"

Just then a white-haired woman in a purple jogging suit a couple seats down turned to DJ and said, "You won, dear."

"I won?" DJ knew she looked shocked. And she was worried the security guard was about to come over and read her rights to her. But he was just talking to someone else, maybe an undercover guard.

"Not bad," said the woman. "That's $500."

"$500?" DJ looked at her with wide eyes. "How do you know?"

So the woman got up and came over and pointed to the amount. "See?"

"Oh, yeah." DJ stared at the total. "So ... where's the money?"

The woman laughed. "Is this the first time you've played slots?"

DJ nodded.

"Are you finished?"

DJ nodded again.

"Push that button."

So DJ pushed it, and, after a few very long seconds, a little white slip of paper popped out. "That's it?" asked DJ with disappointment.

"That's not bad for your first time." The woman shook her head and returned to her machine and pushed the button again.

"Thanks," said DJ quickly. Then, glancing over at the security guy who was still talking to the suit, DJ slipped down another aisle of slot machines and then hurried directly to the elevators. Feeling like a bandit and slightly giddy, she rode up and practically ran to the suite.

"What's wrong with you?" asked Taylor when DJ walked through the living room and straight to the kitchen area.

DJ didn't say anything. She opened the fridge and pulled out a bottle of water, then took a long swig.

"What happened to you?" asked Eliza. "You're all flushed. Did someone mug you or something?"

DJ went over to the sectional and flopped down. "More like the opposite," she said.

"You *mugged* someone?" asked Eliza.

DJ actually laughed now. "Not exactly, but you're getting warmer."

"What is going on with you?" demanded Taylor. "I thought maybe you'd gone to the airport to fly back home. You were so ticked at me last night."

"I was trying to change my flight."

"Any luck?" asked Eliza with too much interest.

DJ rolled her eyes. "Yeah, right."

"So what are you all excited about?" Taylor sat next to DJ and stared at her. "What happened?"

DJ opened her bag and pulled out her little white slip of paper and handed it to Taylor. Then Eliza leaned over the back of the couch and looked at it too.

"$500?" Taylor frowned. "How'd you get this?"

"Did you steal it?" Eliza's voice sounded accusing.

"Of course not."

Taylor laughed. "You played the slots?"

"Not on purpose."

"By accident?"

"I was just sitting there, so I put in a dollar, and suddenly the machine went nuts."

"And you won?" Eliza's eyes got wide.

DJ nodded and, despite herself, she started giggling. "I thought the security guard was going to card me, so I gave him the slip." Although she'd been scared then, for some reason this seemed incredibly funny now. Soon they were all laughing.

"Way to go, DJ!" Taylor slapped her on the back. "I didn't know you had it in you, girlfriend."

"Yeah," agreed Eliza. "I heard they're pretty careful about minors gambling. You really could've gotten into trouble."

"So what do I do with it now?" asked DJ, suddenly worried again. "Maybe I should give it back—"

"Give it back?" said Taylor. "Are you nuts?"

"Well, it's wrong. I am underage."

"But the casino takes millions away from people every day. Why would you give it back?" Taylor shoved the ticket back at DJ.

DJ looked down at the ticket. To be honest, she wasn't even sure what the right thing to do was.

"If you're that worried about it," said Eliza, "just spend it at the hotel while you're here—then they get it back anyway."

"That's right," agreed Taylor. "There's a great shoe store."

Eliza laughed. "Yes! Buy shoes."

"But how do I get the money from the ticket?" asked DJ. "Won't they figure out that I'm not twenty-one?"

"They have a machine."

"But what if they see—"

139

"Never mind," said Taylor. "I'll get it for you." She pulled DJ to her feet. "Let's go."

DJ went back to the casino with them but stood on the sidelines and pretended not to watch as Taylor and Eliza walked over to the payoff machine. Then, cool as a cucumber, Taylor came back and slipped DJ the stack of twenties as they walked over the café to get some breakfast.

"Should I count them?" asked DJ.

Taylor laughed, and DJ stuck the money in her bag. Still, she felt like a thief. Okay, a slightly giddy thief.

As they ate breakfast, DJ sensed that something about the dynamics between the three of them had changed. There no longer seemed to be a sense of competition between them, and it was almost like they were having fun. So when Eliza announced she was ready for the pool, DJ didn't even argue. Besides, after her cheese and bacon omelet, she knew it would feel good to swim some laps.

Of course, it slowly turned into the same old, same old when Eliza and Taylor began playing hostesses to the hottest cabana party at the pool. And Arden and Tony both seemed to enjoy being the "favored" guests, which wasn't saying much since the pool was relatively quiet. Probably because tomorrow was Christmas Eve and most people had better places to be. But by midafternoon, DJ was bored. Still, she decided not to be bratty about it. She simply told Taylor that she wanted to find something more interesting to do. "I just want to have fun," she said. "Plain old fun."

"Doing what?" asked Eliza, who had been listening.

DJ shrugged. "Anything." She glanced over to where Tony was indulging in what must've been his sixth beer. "This just isn't fun."

"I know," agreed Eliza. "I'm ready to ditch these dudes."

"Me too," said Taylor. Then without batting an eyelash, Taylor announced. "We have to go now." She patted her hair. "Salon appointments." Then they grabbed up their pool stuff and made a quick exit with the guys calling after them, asking when could they meet up again.

"Later," called Taylor. DJ just giggled. And Eliza gave them a finger wave. On the way up in the elevator, Eliza asked what they should do next.

"It has to be something fun," said DJ.

"Okay," agreed Taylor. "Fun it is."

DJ felt hopeful. "Let's all agree to make this a total fun day—just girls having fun. Good, clean fun, okay?"

"Okay," agreed Eliza. "I'm in. A totally fun day."

"With no guys ..." Taylor seemed to be mulling this over.

"I know!" said Eliza. "Let's be French for a day."

"Huh?" DJ frowned.

"I used to do this with a friend, and it's hilarious. We'll dress up—haute couture—and stroll around the casino, speaking only French and acting very French, which means we look down on everyone."

DJ considered this. *Everyone* included guys, and she was sick of the way guys had been hitting on them. "Works for me," said DJ. "But my French is pretty bad. I only had one year before I switched to Spanish."

"Well, mine is excellent," said Eliza, already putting on a believable French accent.

"And mine will pass," said Taylor. Then she said something in French that DJ only partially understood, and Eliza laughed. "And we will go to Paris," announced Taylor as they emerged from the elevator.

"Huh?" DJ was confused now.

But, after they were dressed—*tres chic*—they did go to Paris. Paris, the casino. They were transported there in a stretch Hummer, and when they stepped out of it, they were already in character. Each emerged slowly and elegantly from the vehicle, taking her time and holding her head high, with that bored expression that both Taylor and Eliza had tutored DJ about—although DJ was now Desiree. She could feel eyes on the three of them as they stood in front of the hotel, conversing casually amongst themselves in French.

"Who are they?" asked a middle-aged woman in capri pants.

"I don't know," said her friend. "But they seem familiar."

"A French music group?" suggested the man with them.

DJ had to control herself from laughing as they walked past the onlookers with heads held high.

"Fashion models," whispered a woman. "I can tell by the way they walk. Look at the dark-haired one in the middle. I'm sure I've seen her on one of those model shows on TV."

And that's pretty much the way it went. Everywhere the striking French threesome went, they were sure to get looks and—once people decided they only spoke French—comments. And some of the comments were hilarious. DJ really was having fun. Okay, it was a warped sort of fun, but, hey, it was Vegas.

They did some shopping, not too much, but enough that they each had an impressive (but not too heavy) bag to tote along. Finally, Eliza announced in French that she was hungry and that she was treating them to dinner at the Eiffel Tower.

"*Non reservations?*" questioned DJ.

"Desiree, Desiree . . ." Eliza just smiled and told her not to worry.

But when they got there, the maitre d' asked if they had reservations. That's when Eliza took over in a heavy French accent. "Do you not know who I am?"

He looked at her, then shook his head.

She frowned prettily. "Ooh, I am so devastated. Surely, you know who I am, do you not?"

"Paris Hilton?" he ventured, and DJ almost choked, but managed to keep her face blank as she patted the back of her hair, still smooth in the sleek French twist that Taylor had fixed for her.

"No!" Eliza turned to DJ and Taylor now, speaking in rapid French. And DJ followed Taylor's lead by frowning and shaking her head. "We will go!" Eliza said loudly, "to where we are known and appreciated." She pointed out the window. "Bellagio!"

"Wait, wait," said another man who had joined the flustered maitre d'. "We have your table ready, ladies." He held up three menus. Then, speaking in French, he invited them to follow him as he led them to what must've been the best table in the restaurant. Then he apologized, still in French, to Eliza. After that they were treated like celebrities and even given a complementary bottle of Pinot Noir.

"You have to at least taste it," whispered Taylor as she poured a small amount into DJ's glass. "Or pretend."

"Or else they might wonder," Eliza said quietly, "and check ID."

Taylor held up her glass for a toast, reverting back to French now, and they all dinged glasses. DJ took a cautious sip — just to be congenial. But that was all. The truth was, besides not wanting to break the law, she didn't like the taste of alcohol. So why bother?

Eliza ordered for everyone in perfect French, and the food seemed to keep coming all evening. DJ sampled an *escargot*, a snail, but decided it wasn't her favorite. Everything else was very good. Plus the view of the Bellagio fountains lit up in the night was gorgeous. They even ordered coffee and desserts, which they shared.

DJ had to admit this was really quite fun. Okay, it was expensive fun, but it was Eliza's money. DJ knew that this day could've gone a lot worse. She also knew that this day was not over. Not by a long shot.

IT WAS NINE BY THE TIME they got back to their suite. They were barely comfortable before both Taylor and Eliza started getting antsy. DJ knew they wanted to go clubbing. They'd already made comments about who was playing where, and what clubs were the best, and it was pretty obvious that it wouldn't be easy to keep these girls home.

"Remember your promise," DJ said as Taylor flipped through the TV channels and stopped at the one that advertised the Vegas hot spots. "We agreed to have fun all day long, just girls having fun."

"But this isn't fun," complained Taylor. "And I want a drink."

"Order room service," suggested Eliza.

Taylor frowned. "My mom doesn't want me ordering alcohol."

DJ was pleasantly surprised.

"I know! I'll order it from my room." And before DJ could protest, Eliza jumped up and ran out. DJ had to think this might be preferable than going to the nightclubs. It might keep Taylor out of trouble for one more night. Eliza too. DJ would not normally have cared, but Eliza had sort of grown on her today. While they waited for Eliza to return, DJ talked Taylor into playing gin rummy. As soon as Eliza showed up with a loaded room service cart in tow—complete with an assortment of drinks and snacks—Taylor was done with cards.

"Come on, DJ," urged Eliza as she held a glass of wine in front of her, "even Jesus drank wine."

"That's right," said Taylor as she refilled her own glass with something that looked a lot stronger than wine. "And he hung with his sinner friends too."

"Just like me," teased DJ.

"Jesus' first miracle was to turn water into wine," pointed out Taylor.

"Yeah, yeah ..." DJ rolled her eyes. "So you've said."

"I know what we can do," said Taylor. "Let's play a game."

"Gin rummy?" asked DJ.

"No ..." Taylor got that sly look. "Truth or dare."

Soon they were immersed in the silly game, starting slowly with the predictable questions about boys and sex and, naturally, DJ's answers were usually disappointing. DJ stayed with "truth" because she was too afraid to take a dare from either of these two girls.

But then it got a little deeper, and Eliza, probably under the influence, actually admitted that she had an insatiable need to be best and first and prettiest in everything. She sniffed. "And you Carter House girls make it very difficult." She refilled her glass. "But I refuse to give up." She gave Taylor and DJ a slightly wicked smile. "Oh, yes, we may be friends, but be forewarned, I will fight both of you to the bitter end." Then she threw back her head and laughed like she was joking. But DJ was pretty sure it was the truth.

Now it was Taylor's turn. "Okay." Eliza rubbed her hands together with a sly look. "Let me do this one, DJ. I've got a really good question for the wild child. Truth or dare, Taylor?"

Taylor narrowed her eyes like she was weighing her options, then finally said, "Dare."

Eliza was clearly disappointed, and DJ was curious about what her question would've been.

"Are you sure?" Eliza asked Taylor.

But Taylor just nodded and took another long swig. "Go for it."

"Okay," said Eliza in a devious tone, "but you may want to change your mind when you hear the dare."

"I doubt it."

"All right. I dare you to strip down to your underwear and walk all the way through the casino and back."

"No way," said DJ. "She'll get arrested."

"This is Vegas," pointed out Eliza. "Besides, she can decline and do truth instead."

But Taylor did not decline. A few minutes later, Eliza wheeled the room service cart out into the hallway and left it by someone else's door. Then, Taylor, despite DJ's pleading, strutted through the crowded casino in her underwear and three-inch heels.

Okay, it was very pretty underwear—hot pink and lacy, and at least she had on panties and not a thong—but it was *still* underwear. DJ watched from the sidelines in horror. Meanwhile, Eliza, keeping a distance of about fifteen feet, appeared to be stalking her. Some people barely seemed to notice the gorgeous scantily clad girl. But they were in Vegas after all—they'd probably seen it all. And other onlookers, mostly guys, hooted and clapped and asked for phone numbers and dates. But even the security guards seemed blasé. DJ wondered what they'd do if Taylor was naked.

Finally, it was over, and DJ wished she'd thought to bring down a bathrobe or something. But she felt it took all she had to keep up with these two. Really, Taylor and Eliza were like gasoline and matches—a dangerous and potentially explosive combination. If only DJ could be the fire extinguisher to put their fires out—or just keep them at a safe distance.

Then, just when DJ was about to let out a sigh of relief, two thirty-something couples got into the elevator with them. They all took one shocked look at Taylor and looked away. Except that the men looked back, and the women looked like they wanted to hit somebody—either their men or Taylor. DJ wasn't sure.

But when the elevator stopped on the twenty-third floor so the two couples could get off, Taylor, in her most seductive voice said, "What happens in Vegas ... stays in Vegas." One of the women turned around and gave Taylor a discrete but intense middle-finger salute. Then, as the doors closed, Eliza burst into giggles, Taylor sighed as if bored, and DJ just shook her head. Really, it was hopeless.

It was nearly eleven by the time they were back in their room and Taylor had put her clothes back on. But that little escapade must have reenergized the crazy pair, because it seemed that Eliza and Taylor were just warming up. They begged DJ to go down with them, but she told them, "No way," and reminded them that they had promised a girls' day of fun.

"But it's nighttime now," said Taylor as she reached for her new Kate Spade bag.

"And soon it will be tomorrow," said Eliza as she stood by the mirror near the door and touched up her mascara. "And this is Vegas, dahling, the town that never sleeps."

DJ knew there was no stopping them, besides she was too tired to even try. At least Taylor wouldn't be alone tonight. Not that Eliza was a great comfort.

"Hurry," said Taylor. "My mom will be back any minute."

And just like that they were gone. DJ went to bed. Before she went to sleep, she prayed, asking God to keep the two foolish girls safe. Then she asked God to help her make it through tomorrow and Christmas. She finally said a weary, "amen," and then just before drifting to sleep she added on a P.S. as if she'd been writing a letter. "And, if you're not too busy, God, maybe you can find me a quicker way to get back home. Thanks."

The next morning, DJ was shocked to discover that Taylor wasn't in her bed. Plus her bed hadn't been slept in. But then she remembered Eliza and figured Taylor must've stayed in her room. At least she hoped so. Just the same, DJ didn't want to run into Eva this morning. She didn't want to have to play Miss Congeniality. Or to explain her missing daughter. She didn't want to lie either. So, without even showering, DJ pulled on yesterday's sweats and grabbed her bag and slipped out of the quiet suite.

Once again, she went to Starbucks. She ordered a mocha and a blueberry muffin, then found a soft leather chair in a corner and made herself comfortable. She wished she could hide out there all day and pretend Taylor and Eliza didn't exist. However, she left her cell phone on just in case.

By noon no one had called. DJ was tempted to call Casey just to complain. But she could imagine how Casey would lay into her for being such a fool. To meet Taylor in Vegas *and* have Eliza pop in? No, that was too humiliating. Finally, DJ decided to go check on her friends. Hopefully they hadn't been abducted by nasty old men or aliens last night. As soon as she went into the suite, she realized her mistake.

"Oh, there you are," said Eva a bit too eagerly.

"Good morning." DJ forced a smile.

"Where is Taylor?"

DJ glanced over to the bedroom she and Taylor shared. The door was open and DJ had left it closed.

"I can see she's been out all night."

"Yes." DJ nodded. "But I think she's with Eliza."

"Eliza?"

So DJ quickly explained, and Eva seemed notably relieved. "Tell Taylor that I'd like to meet Eliza."

"I will. Although she leaves on a red-eye flight for Paris tonight. That's where her family is spending Christmas. They have an estate there."

"Oh."

"But I'll tell her." Then DJ went into the room, put on her swimsuit, and got her pool things. Before she headed down to the pool, she knocked on Eliza's door. No answer. She knocked louder. "Eliza!" she called, "Open up!"

A housekeeper paused, looking at DJ. "Did you forget your key?"

"Yes," said DJ. "I was heading to the pool and—"

"Let me help." And just like that, the maid waved her magic card through the door and DJ walked in. Although she felt guilty for lying, she also felt desperate. She thanked the maid, entered the suite, and closed the door. It was similar to Eva's suite, but with only one bedroom. She tiptoed toward the bedroom, preparing herself for anything.

But to her relief, Taylor and Eliza, still fully clothed, were on top of the queen beds. Probably passed out. DJ paused long enough to be sure they were still breathing, and she considered tossing a blanket over them, but thought why bother? It's not like they took their health seriously. Then, without saying a word, she slipped back out.

"Everything okay?" asked the maid.

"Just fine. Thanks." She considered putting a Do Not Disturb sign on the door, but if anyone deserved to be disturbed, it seemed like those two had it coming. For the next few hours, DJ swam laps, sunned, read her book, got a nice late lunch, which she ate poolside in the cabana, and took a nice little nap. She enjoyed herself. Really, she wondered, what was wrong with that? Once again she had to question what was it about drinking, flirting, and clubbing that was so enticing to some girls? Was it worth the risks? And what about the hangovers? Really, it seemed totally crazy.

By the time DJ returned from the pool, it seemed that her friends were in agreement. Somehow Eliza and Taylor managed to make it back to Eva's suite, but they both still looked a little green around the gills.

"I'm not going to do that again," Eliza assured DJ as she held a cold washcloth to her forehead.

"At least not real soon?" DJ couldn't help but be skeptical. But Eliza didn't respond. Taylor was in the bedroom, sitting on the edge of the bed with a blank look on her face. "Are we having fun yet?" teased DJ.

Taylor threw a flip-flop at her. Then DJ went out to discover that Eliza was heading for the door. "Tell Taylor I'll be in my suite," she muttered as she shuffled out. "I thought I felt better, but now I'm not so sure ..."

At around six that evening, both Taylor and Eliza rallied. "Let's get something to eat," suggested Taylor.

"Maybe some soup," said Eliza tentatively.

"Or a big thick steak," said DJ dramatically, "bloody rare."

Eliza made a face and turned away, but DJ just laughed. She wasn't being very nice, but she was only trying to remind Eliza of her stupidity. To drive the point home.

"I think I'll have a steak too," said Taylor as they rode down the elevator. "And maybe some fried eggs on top, real greasy and—"

"Shut up!" Eliza leaned against the elevator wall. "Or I'll hurl on both of you. I swear I will."

Taylor just laughed. But neither of them made any more food jokes.

"You must have a cast-iron stomach," said Eliza to Taylor as they walked through the casino toward the restaurant. No one ordered drinks with dinner, which DJ took as a good sign. After her soup, Eliza felt well enough to indulge in a salad too. Meanwhile, Taylor and DJ indulged in rib eye steaks.

"I really wanted to see your mom perform," said Eliza as they were finishing.

"She's on tonight at 7:30," said Taylor. "Knock yourself out."

"Really? Can we still get tickets?"

Taylor just rolled her eyes. "I'm not going. But I can get you a ticket if you really want to."

"Please, come," urged Eliza. "Both of you."

"I'm happy to go." DJ agreed for two reasons. For one thing, she really liked Eva's voice. Besides that, it was a way to keep these girls out of the clubs. Although she suspected that Eliza wouldn't be tempted tonight.

"You two can go," said Taylor as she signed the check. "I'll get your tickets."

"What about you?"

"There's a good bass player at House of Blues tonight. You can meet up with me there after my mom's concert."

Eliza tried to get Taylor to change her mind, but she refused. "I've seen her a bazillion times. And this bass player is really good." Then Taylor walked them to the theater and secured the tickets as well as backstage passes before she took off. DJ decided not to worry about Taylor as she and Eliza found their seats—once again, down close to the front and in the center. And, once again, the concert was amazing and wonderful. Even Eliza seemed impressed.

"Should we go backstage?" she asked DJ.

"Sure. Eva said she wanted to meet you."

"Me?" said Eliza.

DJ nodded and, acting like she'd done it before, led Eliza back to where an usher brought them to Eva's dressing room. And there, she introduced Eliza. Eva smiled graciously as Eliza gushed about the concert.

"Where's Taylor?" Eva directed this at DJ, but before she could answer, Eliza jumped in.

"She headed out already." Eliza laughed. "I guess going backstage to meet your own mother isn't such a thrill."

Eva laughed, but her eyes remained on DJ, a questioning look and sadness there. DJ forced a weak smile, and then they said good-bye and took off to catch up with Taylor. On the way to the club, DJ warned Eliza that she was not going in.

"Why not?" demanded Eliza.

"For one thing, I'm not old enough. Besides that I don't have fake ID. Furthermore, I don't want fake ID. So tell Taylor I'm going to bed."

Eliza looked disappointed. "Then I'll tell you good-bye now. I'm flying out of here at 12:40 a.m."

DJ looked at her watch. "Do you know that it's half past nine now?"

"I'm aware of the time. My bags are packed, and the limo is scheduled. I'm fine."

"You better not get drunk and miss your flight."

"Thanks, Mom." Then, to DJ's surprise, Eliza hugged her. "It was fun ... well, sometimes."

"Merry Christmas," said DJ.

"To you too." Then Eliza pulled out her fake ID, flashed it to the security guard, and walked into the club. Just like that. Easy breezy. And DJ went up to the suite, got ready for bed, tried to read awhile, but was soon asleep. Easy breezy. But when DJ woke up, it was nearly one in the morning and Taylor was not back. If all had gone well, Eliza should be in the air, which meant that Taylor was down there by herself and probably drinking.

While one part of DJ was totally fed up and didn't care, another part remembered the troubled look in Eva's eyes tonight. So DJ got out of bed, pulled on her sweats, and headed down to the club. Hopefully, Taylor was still there. And hopefully Eliza had made her flight.

DJ hung around the entrance of the club, looking in to see if she could spot Taylor until she was approached by a security guard. "Are you coming in?" he asked.

"No," she said, quickly concocting a plan. "But my friend is here. And she's underage. You let her in with fake ID, and now her dad is coming here, and he's got a cop with him, and there's—"

He unhooked the velvet cord. "Come with me. You point her out, and she's out of here." He was already talking into his little radio device, alerting someone else.

"Thanks," said DJ as they made their way through the crowded room. And there up front on the dance floor, was Taylor, dancing with several guys in a way that would've

154

been considered porn if she'd been dressed like last night. DJ pointed her out. "Her name is Taylor," she told the guy. He relayed this to whoever was listening, then took DJ back out to wait. She looked nervously over her shoulder like she expected the cops any minute. Then another security guy escorted Taylor out and shoved her toward DJ. "You kids stay out of here! You show your face again, I'll be calling the cops." The other guard winked at DJ as she dragged a staggering Taylor away.

IT WAS AFTER TEN by the time DJ woke up the next morning. Taylor, safe in bed, appeared to be sleeping it off as DJ quietly made her way to the bathroom. She took her time in the shower and getting dressed, but Taylor was still sleeping. Big surprise. But DJ could smell coffee, so she went out to see Eva in the kitchen, humming quietly as she poured herself a cup of coffee.

"Good morning," said DJ.

"Oh, good morning, DJ," said Eva. "Did you sleep well?"

"Yes."

"And Taylor?"

"Sleeping like a baby."

Eva smiled sadly. "Yes, she's not a morning girl. But she did get in . . . not too late last night?"

"Not too late."

She nodded. "I'm so glad you came, DJ. Taylor needs a friend like you."

DJ forced a halfhearted smile.

"Help yourself to coffee. My breakfast is on the way. Feel free to order whatever you like."

"Actually, I think I'll go down. I've gotten kind of addicted to Starbucks lately."

"Yes, a friend of mine claims they put something in their coffee." She smiled and picked up the newspaper. "Enjoy."

DJ grabbed her bag. "I have my phone. If Taylor wakes up, she can call me."

"I'll tell her."

DJ went to Starbucks and ordered her regular mocha, this time with a bagel. She decided to call Rhiannon — just for moral support and encouragement. But Rhiannon's phone went straight to messaging. So she tried Casey, determined not to mention that Eliza had been here. When she answered, Casey sounded grumpy.

"What's wrong?" asked DJ.

"My parents."

"You didn't ask them if you could come to Vegas, did you?"

Casey laughed. "No. I'm not stupid. And after I heard about Eliza, well, I'm not insane like some people."

"How did you hear?"

"Rhiannon told me. What a mess."

"Don't rub it in. At least she's gone. Now it's just Taylor."

"Lucky you." Then Casey used a bad word, which really wasn't a good sign.

"What's wrong?"

Casey lowered her voice. "My parents just started World War Three."

"Oh . . . that's too bad."

"Yeah . . . and on Christmas Eve too."

"I'm sorry."

"It's not really anything new . . . I mean, my parents always seem to fight more during holidays than any other time."

"I never knew that." DJ had spent a lot of time in Casey's home while growing up. She always thought of them as a perfect, happy family.

"Well, they don't do it if anyone is around. I mean, besides us kids."

So DJ told Casey about last night's meltdown. "I was so bummed," she admitted. "I'm sure I was feeling envious of you around that time, wishing I was with a normal family, celebrating the holidays with love and good cheer."

Casey laughed with sarcasm. "Talk about a fractured fairy tale."

"Well, it might not be that great, but I think it's better than trying to keep Taylor out of trouble. What a way to spend Christmas!"

"Seems like you would've thought of that sooner."

DJ could tell she wasn't going to get any sympathy from Casey. If anything, it seemed that Casey was still jealous—and grumpy. "Well, hang in there," DJ finally said. "I'll be praying for you."

"Pray for my parents—they're the ones who need it."

DJ closed her phone and shook her head. Was it just her imagination or was the whole world a mess? Were there any "normal" families out there? Ones with genuine love and good will toward each other? Conner seemed to have a decent family—and they were probably having a good time skiing in Montana. And even Eliza, despite her lack of good sense, seemed to have a fairly good family—or maybe it was just an act, the kind that the very wealthy are so clever at putting on.

DJ tried not to feel sorry for herself as she walked through the hotel lobby. Although it was decorated for Christmas, it was too much and over the top—just like everything else in Vegas. Even the Christmas music sounded overdone and gaudy and fake. Really, who spends Christmas in Vegas?

Then she thought of Eva. She was here to work and didn't really have much choice. And, although she was a bit oblivious, she seemed to have some inkling that all was not well with her daughter. And yet what could Eva do? Lock her up? That's when it occurred to DJ that perhaps she could make this Christmas a bit more cheerful for Eva . . . and maybe for Taylor too. Not that Taylor would notice or care.

Suddenly, DJ remembered her slot winnings and her determination to leave it all in Las Vegas. It was time to go Christmas shopping. This turned out to be a challenge since the hotel shops either seemed outrageously expensive or else they catered to the sort of glittery glop that Vegas was so famous for.

After awhile, she finally discovered an elegant shop with some beautiful pieces of hand-blown glass. After browsing for quite some time, she found what she hoped would be appropriate gifts. For Eva, it was a beautiful hand-blown bowl with swirling colors of red, gold, and rust. And for Taylor it was a quirky hand-blown clown figurine. Okay, she wasn't sure if there was some symbolism there, but the clown was actually rather sweet and charming. She got them both wrapped and then selected Christmas cards. Along the way, she saw a florist shop where she stopped to order a festive bouquet of red roses and ivy to be delivered to the suite. Feeling pleased with her finds and her attempt at Christmas spirit, she headed back to the suite.

"Where have you been?" asked Taylor when DJ came into the room.

"Out and about." DJ set her shopping bags on the coffee table.

"Shopping?"

"Maybe."

"Well, you could've left a note or something." Taylor frowned as she tightened the belt on her satin robe. "I had no idea where you'd gone."

DJ controlled herself from pointing out that Taylor had been doing the same thing. "I told your mom I was going to Starbucks and that you could call me if you got up."

"She wasn't here either. She must've already gone to rehearsal. Tonight's and tomorrow's concerts have a Christmas theme, so they needed some extra practice."

"Oh."

"Are you still mad at me?" Taylor gave DJ her most appealing smile. "Or can we let bygones be bygones?"

"What does that really mean anyway?"

"You know, bury the hatchet. Forgive and forget. Start over."

DJ sighed. "I guess so. But just for the record, I get worried about you. And I don't think you should go clubbing alone."

"I wasn't alone. Eliza was with me."

"Her flight was long gone, Taylor. You were dancing with a couple of strange guys—very seductively too."

"You were there?" Taylor looked surprised. "Inside the club?"

"I saw you. Okay?" DJ was mad now. "And it worried me. And your mom's worried too, Taylor. For good reason. What you do is dangerous. Seriously messed up. Don't you get that?"

"I get that you're overreacting."

DJ took a deep breath. She hadn't meant to lose it like this. She'd meant to be kind and gracious. And yet . . .

"Look," she said gently. "I just wish you'd be more careful, Taylor. And I can't help if it's upsetting. Seriously, I'm ready to give you a big lecture about Natalie Holloway and those jerks in Aruba . . . but I won't."

"Thanks for sparing me."

"Well, you don't know what might happen, Taylor. This is Vegas."

"Yes, I'm aware of that."

"And I got to thinking . . . what kind of people spend Christmas in Las Vegas?"

"People like us?"

"Yes, but I'm not talking about us, Taylor. I'm talking about thugs and jerks and losers and abusers—people who are more comfortable with gambling and drinking than being with their families."

"Maybe they don't have families."

"Maybe some of them don't." DJ frowned. Actually, that pretty much described her. But that wasn't her point. Why couldn't Taylor get this? "Don't you ever get scared, Taylor? Don't you have any sense of fear whatsoever?"

Taylor shrugged.

"I mean what if you got into a situation . . . you know, over your head. What if some jerk pulled a knife or gun on you and forced you to go out and get in his car?"

Taylor just laughed. "I would scream my freaking head off."

DJ nodded. "Yeah, well, that would probably help. But what if the guy was really clever? What if he got you somewhere remote before you discovered he was a jerk?"

"I wouldn't be that stupid."

"What if you were drunk, Taylor? What if your senses were impaired?"

"Oh, DJ, you are such a worrywart."

"I just want you to think."

"Sometimes I think you're, like, about forty-five years old."

"Thanks."

"So, let's change the subject." Taylor walked over to the window and looked down. "What are we doing today?"

"I don't know."

"Why don't we start at the pool again ... until we figure out something else."

"Sounds good to me."

As it turned out, they spent most of the day at the pool. And to DJ's relief, Taylor didn't stock the mini fridge with booze this time. And there was no real partying going on in cabana 14. The girls had a late lunch at a poolside café and mostly snoozed and swam and read. In fact, DJ thought maybe things were taking a turn for the better.

"My mom left a message," Taylor informed DJ after she closed her cell phone. "She invited you and me to come to her concert tonight."

"That sounds great."

"Really? This will be, like, your third time. Not to mention two nights in a row?"

"So ... I like her. She's good."

"Okay ..."

And so they dressed up again—not as fancy as on previous nights—and they went to hear Eva's Christmas concert, which was a completely different show thanks to the Christmas numbers. And it was wonderful—even better than the other concert. Then, to DJ's relief, she somehow enticed Taylor to return to the suite. How she would keep her there remained to be seen. "I'm tired." DJ feigned a yawn as they rode the elevator up.

"But it's so early," protested Taylor.

"It's also Christmas Eve," DJ told her. "Wouldn't it be nice to spend it in the suite?"

"I don't know why."

"Maybe your mom will want some company."

"My mom will be exhausted. She has to go to a late dinner, and by the time she gets back, she'll probably go straight to bed."

When they entered the suite, DJ kicked off her shoes and turned on the flat-screen TV. "Maybe we can find an old movie," she said hopefully. She knew that Taylor loved some of the classics.

"I'm hungry," said Taylor. "Why don't we go get something to eat?"

"How about room service?"

"That will take forever."

"How do you know?"

"Trust me, I know."

"Oh . . ." DJ looked around the spacious suite and wondered how she could possibly entice Taylor not to go out. She picked up a pack of cards and held them up. "Maybe we could play cards."

Taylor made a face. But then she seemed to get interested. "Okay, how about some gin rummy?"

DJ brightened. "Yeah, we never did finish our last game."

"Cool." Taylor kicked off her shoes now. "But let's change into comfortable clothes first."

Now DJ was feeling really hopeful and started to go for her sweats, but Taylor shook her head. "No, I mean like jeans."

"What's the difference?"

"For gin rummy."

DJ frowned. "Who cares?"

"To go downstairs."

"Huh?" Now DJ was confused.

"For gin rummy. We can play it downstairs."

"Why?"

"Because it's fun."

DJ was feeling suspicious now. "You mean gambling?"

"No. I don't mean gambling. I know that's risky. I just mean plain old gin rummy. Are you interested or not?"

DJ gave in. She put on her jeans, and the next thing she knew they were walking through the casino again. Finally, Taylor stopped in front of what appeared to be a club. A club DJ hadn't seen. A club called Gin Rummy.

"See," said Taylor. "Gin Rummy."

DJ wanted to smack her.

"Come on," urged Taylor. "They have cards in there."

"But it's a—"

"And, oh yeah, I have something for you."

"What?"

"Merry Christmas!" Taylor grinned and slipped DJ what looked like a driver's license. Fake ID!

"Taylor!" exclaimed DJ. "Where did you—"

"Don't ask . . . don't tell." Taylor grabbed DJ's arm and pulled her up to the security guard who, seeing the card in DJ's hand and one in Taylor's, barely looked and then nodded them both through.

"See," said Taylor. "No big deal."

DJ wanted to scream as Taylor pulled her toward a table. The room was smoky, and the music was loud, and DJ had no idea what she should do. It was one thing to turn in Taylor last night, but how could DJ turn her in now? They had both broken the law. What if they got arrested?

"Come on, DJ," urged Taylor. "Pretend this is a Christmas present to me. Let's just hang and have fun, okay? No big deal. And I promise I won't get drunk. Okay?"

"One hour," seethed DJ. "And then we're going back to the suite."

Taylor nodded. "You got it."

But before that hour was even up, Taylor had consumed several rum drinks and was now clearly feeling no pain as she danced the salsa with yet another guy. At the rate she was going, DJ figured it would take the law, her mother, or an act of God to get that girl out of here in one piece. Gin rummy—you bet!

17

AS IT Turned Out, maybe it was an act of God. But when the fire alarm in the club went off, it was all DJ could do not to stand up and cheer. Whether there was a fire or not—and she didn't care—the security guards quickly began escorting patrons out of the club. DJ ran over and grabbed Taylor by the hand and pulled her out.

"Where's the fire?" asked Taylor with a slurred voice.

"In the back, I think," said DJ. Okay, not exactly true, but maybe.

"Where we going?" asked Taylor as DJ continued to tug her along.

"To the suite."

"Uh-uh," protested Taylor.

DJ stopped and turned to look at Taylor, her face just inches away. "Look, either you come up to the suite, or I'm calling your mom and telling her that you're wasted."

Taylor frowned then swore. "You're such a buzz-kill."

"Same back at you," said DJ as she grabbed Taylor by the elbow and continued to make her way toward the lobby. The Christmas music was still playing, and the gaudy decorations looked even worse now, but DJ just kept moving. Her only goal was to get Taylor safely upstairs and to bed. "Merry Christmas, bah humbug!" muttered DJ as she punched the elevator button.

"Huh?" Taylor looked at her with blurry eyes.

"Never mind!"

As they got out of the elevator, Taylor began to sing in a loud slurred voice. "We wiss you a merry Chrish-mush. We wiss you a merry Chrish-mush and a hap—"

"Shh!" DJ put her forefinger over her lips. "People might be sleeping."

"Nobody sleeps in Vegas."

"Your mother might be sleeping," said DJ as she slipped the key card into the door. That seemed to work, because Taylor tiptoed quietly, yet dramatically, into the suite. She headed straight for their room and collapsed on DJ's bed with her clothes on. DJ just shook her head. For this she should get combat pay.

DJ got up around nine the next morning. Taylor was still asleep, snoring loudly, and fully dressed on top of what had been DJ's bed.

"Merry Christmas," said DJ as she tossed her still-warm comforter over Taylor. DJ peeked out to see that the suite was quiet, and she guessed that Eva was sleeping in also. All those performances and rehearsals and late dinner parties had to be exhausting. DJ stretched and looked out the window to the pools below. Another sunny day in "paradise."

She decided to make the most of it by swimming laps. Swim team season was over, but she wanted to stay in shape for spring soccer. So she slipped into her team suit (no bikinis this morning) and went down for a hearty workout. There were a few people lounging around the pool, but for the most part it was pretty quiet. And why not? How many people spent Christmas morning out by a Vegas pool? Crazy.

As she swam, a calmness washed over her. She felt the assurance that, despite the craziness of being in Vegas for Christmas, she was in the right place at the right time. And she had the sense that somehow God was at work. Finally, satisfied with her efforts, she climbed out, wrapped the pool towel around her, and sat down to soak up some morning sun.

"Nice swimming," said a male voice from behind her.

She turned to see an attractive African American guy smiling her way. "Thanks," she told him. "It felt good."

"You must be an athlete."

She nodded. "I'd like to think that I am, but I'm getting over an injury that's slowed me down a little."

"Didn't seem to slow down your swimming." Now he closed the book he'd been reading and set it beside him. She couldn't help but stare at the cover. "Is that a Bible?" she asked.

He grinned. "Yeah. That probably seems weird, huh?"

"No ... just kind of unexpected. I mean, to be reading a Bible in Vegas ... well, it's just not the norm."

"No, I guess not."

"So, are you a Christian?"

His smile grew bigger. "Yeah, I am."

"Cool!"

"How about you?"

"I am too. I just never expected to see another Christian here."

"So, what are you doing here?"

"Trying to help a friend ..." She shook her head. "A friend who doesn't really want my help. How about you?"

"I'm here with my dad. It's his fiftieth birthday this week, and this is where he wanted to spend it." He sighed like he didn't get it. "But then my dad's not a Christian. My parents divorced a few years ago, and I've been trying to get through to my dad. I thought agreeing to do this with him might help."

"Is it?"

He shrugged. "Hard to tell. Maybe … maybe in time."

"Yeah, maybe with my friend too."

Now he stood up and extended his hand. "Excuse my manners. My name is Terrence Stevenson."

"I'm DJ Lane." She shook his hand. "Nice to meet you. I don't feel quite so alone now."

"For a crowded place, Vegas can feel lonely."

"You got that right."

"What's your friend's name?" he asked. "Maybe I can pray for her."

"Taylor."

He nodded as if making a mental note.

"How about your dad?"

"Reggie."

DJ peered up at the sky. "I wonder what time it is."

"A little past eleven."

"Thanks. I should probably get back. They were asleep when I left, but they could be up by now."

"How long are you here for?"

"Until the 28th … unless I can get an earlier flight."

"Well, maybe I'll see you around then."

DJ stood. "Hey, maybe we can plan to meet up. I mean, my friend Taylor, well, she's pretty into guys … not like I'm trying to set anything up. But it would be interesting to have her meet, well, a Christian guy. It might give her something to think about."

"Sure. That'd be cool."

So they exchanged cell phone numbers, and he told her to call anytime.

"Merry Christmas," she said.

"You too. And remember God really can work in some mysterious ways. Even in Vegas."

"Thanks . . . I'll keep that in mind."

Eva was sitting in the living room when DJ walked in. "Oh, you're up already? I thought both you girls were sleeping in."

"I went down for a swim, but Taylor's probably still sleeping."

She nodded toward the cheerful arrangement of roses and ivy on the coffee table. "Thank you for the flowers, DJ. They're beautiful. And it seems more Christmassy in here."

"You're welcome." Then DJ remembered her gift. "I have something else too." So she hurried and got the package and handed it to Eva. "It's not much."

"Oh, you shouldn't have. I didn't get anything for you."

"Just having me as your guest . . . and hearing your concerts . . . that's a huge gift."

Eva took her time unwrapping the box and peeling the layers of tissue away from the bowl. "Oh, DJ, it's beautiful. The colors are lovely. Thank you."

"You're welcome." DJ grinned happily.

"Your mother must be so proud of you."

DJ's grin evaporated.

Now Eva got a thoughtful frown. "I just remembered something . . . your mother . . . she's passed on, right?"

DJ nodded.

"Just the same, she must feel proud in heaven, DJ, to know she raised such a fine daughter."

"Thanks . . ." DJ looked down at her soggy towel. "I think I'll go catch a shower before Taylor gets up."

"Yes, you do that. I think I'll order up a big Christmas breakfast for all of us. Do you have any special requests?"

"Anything edible," said DJ. "I'm starving."

Eva laughed. "It will be here shortly."

DJ was surprised to see that Taylor had gotten up. But when she found Taylor wrapped around the toilet, she knew what had gotten her up. "Worshiping the porcelain throne again?"

"Go away."

"Sorry," said DJ as she leaned against the vanity and looked at Taylor's hunched form. She had stripped down to her underwear, some very expensive lacy pieces that didn't look too warm. "Anything I can get for you?"

"No. Just leave me alone."

"Mind if I hop in the shower?"

Taylor didn't answer, just groaned. So DJ took this as permission. First she draped one of the thick white bathrobes over Taylor's shoulders. Then she took a quick shower, and got out in time to hear Taylor heaving again. DJ dried quickly and pulled on the other thick bathrobe and then headed to the kitchen to see if she could find something to soothe Taylor's hangover.

She found some ginger ale, which she diluted with water and took back to the bathroom. Taylor was sitting on the toilet lid now, her head bent down and hair straggling all over. DJ found a barrette and managed to pull back some of the wild hair. Then she ran cool water over a washcloth, squeezed it, then handed it to Taylor. Taylor sighed and used the cloth to wipe off her face. "Thanks," she muttered.

"Here," said DJ. "Maybe you can drink a little of this. I'm sure you're dehydrated."

Taylor took the drink, studied it, then took a cautious swig and looked up with what seemed like tears in her eyes. "Why are you being nice to me?"

DJ smiled. "It's Christmas."

Taylor just nodded and took another small sip.

"Can I get you anything else?" offered DJ.

"A replacement for my head?"

DJ suppressed a laugh. Actually, that sounded like a good idea. "I'm going to get dressed. Yell, if you need something."

"I won't be yelling."

By the time DJ was dressed, Taylor had managed to make her way back to the bedroom, landing in her own bed this time. Still in her underwear, she was shivering now. DJ retrieved the comforter and placed it over her.

"My head is on fire," muttered Taylor.

So DJ went back for the cool washcloth and placed it on Taylor's forehead. Then, noticing that Taylor had finished the soda, DJ went to fetch her another one.

"Is Taylor up?" asked Eva as DJ opened the fridge.

"She's up . . . but not feeling too well." DJ took the remaining portion of ginger ale and filled the glass.

Eva nodded sadly. "Hangover?"

DJ was only slightly surprised. "Yeah . . . I guess."

Eva pressed her lips together, then turned away. DJ knew this must be hard on her. It was hard on everyone. And, okay, to be fair, it was hard on Taylor too. DJ took the soda back to the bedroom, but Taylor seemed to have fallen asleep again. So she set it on the bedside table and left.

"I do not know what to do about Taylor," said Eva as DJ rejoined her on the sectional. "I had hoped that her moving to Connecticut would change this . . . this crazy behavior. But I'm afraid that Taylor is too much like her father."

"Is he still at Betty Ford?"

She shook her head. "No, he's out. He's visiting his brother in Florida. And as far as I know, he's doing okay. But it usually takes a few months before he falls off the wagon again."

"Too bad."

"Yes ... terrible waste."

It wasn't long before their breakfast arrived and, as Eva promised, it was a feast. Eva turned on the TV, flipping around until she located an old Christmas movie that DJ had never seen before. And so they watched and ate. And although DJ stuffed herself, and Eva seemed to have a hearty appetite, there was still lots of food left over. So DJ packaged up what looked like it might keep and put the remains in the fridge. Who knew? Taylor might regain her appetite again.

"I know I must seem a party pooper," said Eva, "but if you'll excuse me, I think I will have a nap. I'm still worn out from last night."

"I understand totally," said DJ.

"You just make yourself at home."

"Thanks."

DJ decided to call Grandmother and wish her a Merry Christmas. She hadn't spoken to her since arriving in Vegas. Grandmother sounded as if she was distracted, or perhaps she was on her way to the general's, and so DJ cut the conversation short. Then she turned on the TV again and flipped channels until she found an old episode of Seinfeld that put her straight to sleep.

"Wake up, sleepyhead," said a female voice.

DJ opened her eyes, then blinked to see that Taylor was up and dressed and looking surprisingly well, considering the last time DJ had seen her.

"Merry Christmas." Taylor pointed to DJ's face. "Wipe that drool off your cheek, and let's go get something to eat."

DJ used the sleeve of her shirt to dry her cheek, then sat up. "What time is it anyway?"

"About four."

"There's food in the fridge."

"I don't want leftovers." She grabbed DJ's hand. "Come on. Let's go get a bowl of soup or a salad or something." Thinking it couldn't be too risky to get soup in the middle of the day, DJ agreed. And once they were seated at the restaurant, Taylor actually apologized for getting wasted.

"You know, I didn't really mean to do that. But things got out of hand."

DJ pointed her spoon at her. "See, that's what I was trying to warn you about."

Taylor didn't say anything, but she nodded as if considering this. After they ate, they walked around a bit and got coffees, but the hotel seemed deader than usual. Finally they went back to the suite, where Eva was just getting ready to head out for her show.

"Merry Christmas, darling," Eva said to Taylor, kissing her on the cheek. "I hope you're feeling better."

Taylor tossed DJ a look, then smiled at her mother. "I feel great. Have a good show."

And when it was just the two of them, Taylor turned to DJ and scowled. "Did you tell my mom I was wasted?"

"I didn't have to tell her anything."

"But you didn't cover for me?"

"How was I supposed to do that? Furthermore, why *should* I do that?"

"I thought you were my friend."

DJ pressed her lips tightly together, holding in the angry words she wanted to shoot like bullets at Taylor. Who was Taylor to talk about friends? What kind of friend was she? But yelling at her would be pointless. Especially since she was now storming off to the bedroom, slamming the door behind her. Merry Christmas!

"WHY are you dressed like that?" asked DJ when Taylor emerged about an hour later. She had on a short black skirt, tall boots, and a lacy pink top with a plunging neckline.

"Like what?" asked Taylor, doing a little turn like she thought she was on the runway.

"Like a hooker."

Taylor scowled. "I don't look like a hooker. I just look hot."

"Why do you want to look hot?"

"Because I'm going out."

Part of DJ was ready to barricade the door and put up her fists. She could probably take Taylor. But another part of her simply didn't care. If Taylor wanted to ruin her life like this, why not let her. But instead of doing either of these things, DJ bowed her head and silently prayed.

"What's wrong with you?" asked Taylor as she grabbed up her bag. "Are you sick or something?"

DJ kept her head down. At least she'd gotten Taylor's attention, even if it was only briefly.

"DJ?"

DJ kept her head down, praying fiercely now, asking God to do something—anything—to change this situation. As she was praying, tears started welling up in her eyes. DJ hated to cry—specially in front of someone like Taylor—but the tears were already escaping. Without looking up, DJ used her hands to wipe her cheeks.

"What's wrong?" asked Taylor, now sitting beside her on the sectional.

DJ looked up at Taylor. She had even more tears running down her face now, but suddenly it made no difference. "I *care* about you, Taylor. That's what's wrong. And then you go and say I'm not a good friend. I'm doing everything I can think of to be a good friend, and it's like you just throw it back in my face."

Taylor didn't say anything.

"Who treats their friends like that, Taylor?"

Taylor looked uncomfortable, but she still kept her mouth shut.

"I don't think you even know how to be a friend. Because no matter how hard I try, you push me away. You act like you want a friend, and then you rip the rug out from under me. All I want to know is ... *why*?"

Taylor still wasn't talking.

"I mean, you're an intelligent person. And you can be pretty charming when you want to. You're witty, and sometimes you even show a streak of kindness—occasionally—but then you take it all back. Why do you do that?"

"I don't know."

"You *have* to know. It's like something is eating away inside of you. It's like you *want* to self-destruct. And sometimes it seems like you want to take me along with you—like you think I might enjoy the ride. And I'm just not going there. Do you understand? My life is worth something to me. And maybe I'm not doing that great of a job at it, but I'm trying to be a Christian. And I think God has some better plans for me than getting wasted and ruined and destroyed. And I can't believe you'd settle for that yourself, Taylor. You seem too smart to be like that. And yet you keep disappointing me. *Why?*"

"Do you really want to know?"

"Of course, I want to know!"

Taylor stood, and DJ felt pretty sure that was it. She was going to walk out—just like that. No big deal. Instead, she went to the kitchen and returned with a couple of sodas, handed one to DJ, then wiped the other one across her forehead like she still had a headache.

"It's a long story."

"I'm not going anywhere." DJ popped open the can. "And from what I can see, it's going to be a long night."

And so Taylor finally began to talk. She started by saying she used to be a fairly average girl. "Oh, I knew I was pretty smart. And my mom was a celebrity. But that wasn't so special in the school I attended. It's not like I really stood out that much. I mean, even being mixed racially wasn't a big deal. Not really. For the most part I was pretty normal."

DJ had difficulty envisioning Taylor as "normal."

"I had a best friend." Taylor took a swig. "Jessalyn Dougherty. We were closer than sisters from about second grade until middle school."

"Uh-huh?"

"Jessalyn was so cool. I mean it's like she was perfect."

"No one is perfect."

Taylor narrowed her eyes. "You didn't know her."

"Okay, tell me about her. What made her perfect?"

"She was genuinely good. And kind. She was the kind of girl who would help anyone. She'd give away her lunch. Or she'd be nice to someone who was picked on. She was an honest-to-goodness . . . angel."

DJ tried to imagine this. Taylor (devil girl) and an angel? Interesting.

"And then she got sick."

"Sick?"

"Leukemia."

"Oh."

"The really bad kind." Taylor took another long swig. "Her parents took her all over the country, trying to find help . . . but she died when she was just twelve."

"I'm sorry."

Taylor was crying now, and DJ was unsure what to do. Just the same, she reached her hand over and placed it on Taylor's forearm. A small gesture, perhaps, but something.

"When Jessalyn died, it was like I died too. It's like I couldn't get over it. I mean, I knew that others were hurting too, but I was crushed . . . brokenhearted. My grandmother, as you know, was a strong Christian. She told me that Jessalyn was in heaven, but I didn't want her to be in heaven. I wanted her to be with me. I needed her."

"I know it's hard to lose someone you love, Taylor. You get that I understand that, don't you?"

Taylor nodded and sniffed. DJ went for a box of tissues—for both of them. Then she waited because it seemed there was more to this story.

"My grandmother tried to comfort me. She told me not to be mad at God. And I tried. But about the time I started high school, my grandmother died too—a stroke."

"That must've been hard."

She nodded. "And then I really did get angry at God. But I wasn't really rebelling yet. Not like I would do later—like I've been doing now. By then my dad's drinking was getting out of hand. I know it's because he missed his mother and was probably having some big guilt trip. My mom was gone a lot because she was touring again. I was feeling pretty lost."

DJ shook her head. "Wow, it's like your whole world was crumbling."

"But it gets worse." Taylor reached for a fresh tissue. "After losing Jessalyn, I just couldn't seem to make another real best friend. I mean, there were girls I hung with—some that had known Jessalyn too—but things started getting competitive in high school. The boys started paying more attention to me than before. Not that I was paying that much attention to them at that time. Then at the beginning of sophomore year, a girl named Ilsa befriended me. She'd been a casual friend of Jessalyn, and it almost seemed like our memories of Jessalyn had brought us together. I told her all kinds of things—about how depressed I'd been and everything. We got really close. And I began to feel better."

DJ bit her lip, hoping that Taylor wasn't about to tell her that Ilsa had been hit by a car or something. How much more could she take?

"Then Ilsa betrayed me."

"She betrayed you?" DJ felt confused now. "How?"

"There was a guy named Cole who liked both Ilsa and me. Although I think he liked me more. But Ilsa was madly in love with Cole."

"And?"

"Ilsa begged me to go out with this other guy—a senior named Brent. She said he was an old friend of hers . . . and I guess in a way, he was."

"And did you?"

Taylor nodded. "Oh, yeah ... I did. I was all of fifteen, and it was my first date ever. I didn't really like Brent, but I wanted to make Ilsa happy."

"And?"

"And he raped me."

Tears started pouring down DJ's cheeks again. And this time she threw her arms around Taylor and just sobbed. In fact, they both sobbed. "I'm so sorry," said DJ. "That's so horrible." Eventually they both stopped crying, wiped their noses, and just sat there. "Did you go to the police? Did you press charges?"

Taylor kind of laughed, but with no humor. "I was fifteen. My mom was on tour. My dad was checked out. My best friend had set me up. All I wanted to do was to hide ... or die."

"Oh, Taylor."

"I found out later that Brent had tried the very same thing on Ilsa the previous summer. Somehow she got away. But she never told me—never gave me a word of warning. Just acted like Brent was Mr. Cool, and I was so lucky."

"What a witch!"

"But it gets worse."

"How?" demanded DJ. "How can it possibly get worse?"

"Brent went around telling everyone that we'd had sex, acting like I'd wanted it—like I'd asked for it. Suddenly I had a reputation—one that I didn't want. And, guess what?"

"What?"

"Ilsa no longer wanted to be my friend. She treated me like dirt."

"Wow."

"Yeah ... wow." Taylor blew her nose again. "I need a drink."

DJ took in a deep breath. "I get that you *think* you need a drink, but I don't think that's going to help you."

"Why not?"

"Because it's not a real answer."

"Feels like an answer to me."

"No." DJ shook her head. "It's just a numbing device."

"Numbing is good."

"No, it's not good."

Taylor frowned.

"Think about how you felt this morning, Taylor, when you were hugging the toilet. Do you like feeling that way?"

"No."

"We need a better way to deal with stuff."

"You mean God?"

"Yeah, I do." Suddenly DJ remembered the guy reading his Bible at the pool. Terrence! "Hey, how about if I phone a friend."

"Phone a friend? Is this like that hokey game show?"

"No, it's a guy I met at the pool this morning."

Taylor's eyes lit up. "A guy? Is he hot?"

DJ nodded as she reached for her cell. "Totally."

"Sure, go for it."

As DJ dialed, Taylor headed for the bedroom, probably to fix her face. "Hey, this is DJ," she began, "remember at the pool?"

"You bet. What's up?"

"Well, I know it's Christmas, but I was just having an amazing heart-to-heart with my friend. And suddenly we were talking about God and, the truth is, I feel kind of brain-drained and in over my head."

"Want to meet for coffee?"

"Sure."

So it was agreed that the three would meet at Starbucks in twenty minutes. And when DJ told Taylor, she seemed okay with it.

"There he is," said DJ as they approached Starbucks. Terrence was standing by the entrance.

"Wow, he is hot," said Taylor.

"Let me warn you though," said DJ. "He's a Christian."

"Maybe I can convert him."

"To what?" DJ glanced at Taylor with alarm.

"Just kidding," said Taylor.

Introductions were made, and they soon had their coffees and were seated at a quiet table.

"Tell me about yourself, Terrence," said Taylor.

He flashed what looked like a million-dollar smile. "Well, I'm in my second year at a Bible college in LA."

"Bible college?" Taylor frowned. "Wow, you really are serious. Are you going to be a preacher or something?"

"I'm not sure, but I'm open. I'm even considering some kind of missions work. Maybe in Africa."

"Seriously?" Taylor's eyes grew wide. "A missionary."

"Call it what you like," said Terrence. "I just see it as people helping people. I've been over there with my church a couple of times already, and if anyone needs help nowadays, it's our brothers and sisters in some of the war-torn countries in Africa."

"That's cool." Taylor nodded and took a sip of her caramel mocha. "Helping people is cool."

"Very cool," added DJ. "So, Terrence, were you raised in a Christian home? Is that why your faith is so strong?"

He laughed. "Not even close." Then he told them about his family, his parents' broken marriage, his rebellious teen years, and how God finally got hold of him when he was seventeen. "It's like I couldn't keep running and hiding."

"You don't look like the type of guy who would run and hide," observed Taylor.

"Maybe not so that you would notice. But I hid behind things like sports and popularity and hot chicks and cool cars and stuff like that. It was like this big mask I was wearing—a way to keep people at a safe distance."

DJ turned to Taylor. "Hmmm . . . that sounds familiar." Just then, DJ's cell rang. She checked to see who it was and said, "I better take this." So she moved away from the table and answered. "Hey, Case, what's up?"

"Besides living in a battle zone?"

"Your parents still fighting?"

"Well, they're pretending not to. You know, for the younger sibs. But the looks they give each other . . . the little jabs. Not pretty."

"I'm sorry."

"So how's it going with Taylor?"

DJ wasn't sure how much to say. More than anything she wanted to respect Taylor's confidence right now. She didn't want to do anything that made her feel betrayed. "She's okay."

"Meaning she's right next to you and you don't want to sound catty?"

"No, actually she's talking to this cute guy."

"Probably getting ready to go clubbing?"

"No. He's a nice Christian guy."

"Whoa, that sounds all wrong."

"Or all right."

"Okay. I was just curious. Now I'm even more curious."

"Well, I'm sure you'll hear all about it eventually." DJ watched as Taylor and Terrence continued to talk, and she could tell by Taylor's expression that she was really listening—and maybe she was actually getting it.

"I better go," said Casey. "Don't have too much fun without me, okay?"

"Fun is not how I would describe my day."

"Yeah, whatever."

"Merry Christmas!"

"You too."

But as soon as Casey hung up, DJ called Rhiannon. She knew it was probably getting late back east, but she also knew Rhiannon needed to hear this. Plus it gave DJ a good excuse to let Taylor and Terrence speak freely. "Rhiannon," she said quickly, "you're not going to believe this!" Then she poured out part of the story—not so much about Taylor's past, but more about how she was talking to Terrence now.

"See," said Rhiannon happily. "God is at work!"

"Keep praying!"

"Don't worry. I will."

"How's your mom?"

"A little down. But okay."

"Well, I'll keep praying for her."

"Thanks, DJ. And I'll be praying really hard for Taylor tonight. It sounds like God is up to something."

"I'll keep you posted."

As DJ hung up, she hoped Rhiannon was right. It did seem like God was doing some kind of miracle in Taylor. Yet, at the same time, it seemed so totally impossible. Then again, wasn't he supposed to be the God of the impossible?

"YOU'RE GOING WHERE?" demanded DJ after she rejoined Terrence and Taylor at Starbucks. Taylor had just made a declaration that nearly knocked DJ off her chair.

"LA," said Taylor coolly. "As in Los Angeles. You know that rather large city in California? My family has a house down there. I think you used to live not too far—"

"Yeah, yeah." DJ held up her hands to stop her, then turned and frowned at Terrence. "What is going on here? Can you please shed some light on this or translate for me?"

He made an uncomfortable expression, then sort of smiled. "I was just telling Taylor about this place that a friend of mine runs ... a place where people with problems can go to get well."

Suddenly, and for no explainable reason, DJ was imagining a cult. She'd grown up in the Bay Area and was well aware of some of the craziness that went on in certain areas of their state, including Southern California. Also, she questioned what she really knew about this Terrence fellow, except that he was good-looking and had been reading his Bible in public.

What if he was out recruiting beautiful young women for some crazy cult where everyone was forced to wear purple?

"Don't look so worried," said Taylor.

"But I don't get it." DJ peered at Taylor. "What brought this on so suddenly?"

"Terrence and I were talking ... and I'm trying to get real about my life. I'd think that would make you happy, DJ."

"But where are you going exactly? And when? And why? And—"

"Too many questions," said Taylor.

"I want some answers."

"Okay. I'd like to go ASAP."

"ASAP? As in when ASAP?"

"Tomorrow?" Taylor glanced at Terrence with brows raised hopefully.

He shrugged. "I'll see what we can do."

"Tomorrow?" shrieked DJ. "Are you nuts?"

"Well, according to you, I am," said Taylor. "I mean you've mentioned it a time or two as I recall."

"But I so do not get this." DJ looked from Taylor to Terrence then back to Taylor again. "Seriously, Taylor. What has brought this on?"

Taylor looked evenly back at DJ, but now DJ noticed that Taylor's hands were shaking a little. Was she nervous? Was she under some kind of spell? What?

"I admitted to Terrence that I have a serious drinking problem."

DJ nodded slowly. "A serious drinking problem ..."

"Meaning I may be addicted."

"I thought you just drank occasionally," said DJ. "Kind of a binge drinker."

Taylor looked uncomfortably at Terrence, and he seemed to understand, so he kind of took over. "Look, DJ," he began gently. "I told Taylor about how I was pretty much an alcoholic before I gave my life to God."

"I thought you were a teenager," said DJ.

"Teens can be alcoholics," he said calmly.

DJ nodded. "Well, yeah, I guess I know that."

"What you don't know is how much I've been drinking," said Taylor. "Or how often."

"How much? How often?"

"A lot. And daily. Morning, noon, night."

DJ blinked. "How is that possible? I'm your roommate. Wouldn't I know if you were drinking that much?"

"Most of the time I am quite adept at hiding it."

"Except when you go on a binge—like a party?"

"Exactly."

"Oh." DJ was trying to wrap her head around this.

"Terrence told me about a rehab place, and it hit me ... I *need* to go there."

"Just like that?"

"What?" demanded Taylor. "Do you think I should wait?"

"No, no. Of course, not. I think the sooner the better." DJ glanced at Terrence. "But, no offence, Terrence, what do we know about this place?"

"I gave Taylor the name of the website. It's the place I went when I needed help. Their focus is on young adults ... mostly teens. I think the cutoff is twenty-two."

"But is it possible to get in immediately?" asked DJ.

"I'm not positive, but I spoke to Marlin—that's my friend—shortly before Christmas, and he mentioned that things were going slow there now. That's typical this time of year. Then around New Year's it gets busy, and the waiting list starts filling up."

"Oh."

"So, I think … why not beat the rush?" said Taylor. "You know me—I always like to be ahead of the crowd—trendsetter, cutting edge."

DJ rolled her eyes.

"I thought you'd be glad." Taylor looked slightly hurt now, and DJ knew she'd better get herself together over this. What if this was legit? What if this was God's way of intervening in Taylor's life?

"I am glad," DJ said slowly. "Just kind of shocked."

"If you want, I can call Marlin," offered Terrence. "Just to make sure that there's still space available."

"Sure," said Taylor eagerly. So Terrence stepped away from the table and made his call.

"This is just so sudden." DJ looked into Taylor's eyes. "Are you certain you're ready for this?"

"Remember what I looked like this morning?"

DJ nodded.

"And yet I was dying to get a drink just hours later."

DJ nodded again.

"Does that strike you as a bit odd?"

DJ pressed her lips together, replaying the things that Taylor had told her up in the suite. As strange as this all was, it also made sense. "How long have you been drinking like this?"

"Since the rape."

"But we still don't know much about this place," said DJ quietly. "Or Terrence. I mean, he seems nice. But I only met him this morning. What if—"

"We're in luck," said Terrence as he rejoined them.

"Room at the inn?" asked Taylor.

"Yep. Marlin said to go to the website and fill out the forms as soon as you can."

"No time like now." Taylor stood. "My mom has a laptop upstairs." She stuck out her hand to shake Terrence's. "Thanks for your help."

Terrence smiled as he grasped her hand. "DJ's got my number. Maybe we can stay in touch. I'd like to hear how this goes for you."

"Well, you'll know where to find me."

"That's right." He let go of her hand, then turned to DJ. "Sorry if this caught you off guard. That's usually the way stuff like this goes down. Unexpectedly."

"Yeah . . . I guess."

"Come on," urged Taylor, grabbing DJ's arm. "I need to get to work on this."

So they hurried back to the suite, and Taylor disappeared into her mom's room while DJ paced and prayed. Finally, she called Rhiannon. "Sorry, I'm calling so late," she apologized.

"What's up?"

DJ quickly filled in Rhiannon and, to her relief, Rhiannon didn't seem too alarmed. "That's great."

"But we don't know anything about this place."

"Taylor's not stupid," said Rhiannon. "I mean, she does some pretty dumb stuff, but I can't imagine she'll go someplace that's messed up. And won't her mom check it out too?"

"Actually, they've had some experience with rehab places," admitted DJ. "Her dad goes to Betty Ford pretty regularly."

"So you don't need to worry."

"I guess."

"Be thankful, DJ. It sounds like this is exactly what Taylor needs. See, God was at work. He is at work."

So DJ thanked Rhiannon and hung up. Surely, she was right. Besides, it's not like Taylor was DJ's personal responsibility. But for some reason DJ felt like she was. It's like DJ had invested herself in Taylor. She obviously cared about what happened to her. Besides Eva, DJ probably cared more than anyone.

DJ flopped down on the sectional and threw herself into a desperate prayer for Taylor. She asked God to take control, and—if this was a good thing, the right thing—she asked God to open the door to the rehab place. "But if it's wrong," prayed DJ, "please, please, please, close that door, lock it, and throw away the key!"

"I filled in the forms," announced Taylor when she finally emerged from her mom's room. "I hit Send." She gave DJ a nervous smile. "Now I just need to talk to my mom."

"You're sure about this place?" asked DJ. "I mean, I totally agree that you need rehab—I mean, after what you said. But you're sure this is the right place?"

Taylor's brow creased slightly. "It's hard to explain ... but it sort of feels right. Does that make sense?"

"Yeah ... I guess."

But suddenly Taylor was pacing, as if she wasn't so sure. DJ noticed her hands were shaking.

"Taylor ... are you okay?"

Taylor turned and looked at DJ. "You mean besides craving a drink right now?"

"Is that what's troubling you?"

Taylor closed her eyes and clenched her fists, then nodded.

"Are you going to be okay?"

"Could we just go down and get—"

Just then the door opened, and Eva came in. "Oh, you girls aren't out tonight?" she asked as she tossed her bag into a chair, kicked off her shoes, and then collapsed next to DJ on the sectional. "Anyone hungry?"

"We were just about to go down for something." Taylor grabbed up her bag and looked at DJ. "You coming?"

DJ didn't know what to do, but taking Taylor out to drink seemed like a bad idea. "Don't you want to tell your mom something," said DJ quickly.

"What's going on?" asked Eva.

"Nothing." Taylor was making her way to the door now.

"Taylor," said DJ in a firm voice. "Tell your mom what's going on."

Taylor looked angry now, and DJ knew this could easily go sideways. She shot up a quick prayer.

"What is it, sweetie?" asked Eva in a kind voice. "Is something wrong?"

Taylor came back over and dropped her bag on the floor, then slumped into a chair directly across from them. "I don't know."

"What?" persisted Eva.

Taylor leaned her head back and closed her eyes, emitting a long, weary sigh. "DJ?" she muttered. "Can you tell her?"

Eva turned to stare at DJ now. "What's going on?"

"Well ..." DJ tried to think of where to begin. "I think you know that Taylor drinks."

"Yes?" Eva glanced nervously at Taylor, who was still slumped back with eyes closed. "Did she get into trouble?"

"No." DJ shook her head. "Not yet."

"Oh." Eva looked relieved.

"But she will get into trouble," continued DJ, "if she doesn't get help."

"But she doesn't want help," said Eva.

"Maybe she didn't before … but she does now."

Taylor sat up and stared at her mom. "Let's cut to the chase. I registered myself to go into rehab. It's an inpatient treatment center outside of LA. They have an opening now, and if you give permission, I can enter tomorrow."

"Tomorrow?" Eva blinked, then turned to DJ. "Did you set this up?"

"No."

"I set it up, Mom. I met a guy—through DJ—and he told me about this place, and it just clicked. I knew that I needed help."

"Really?" Eva looked stunned and not entirely pleased. Or maybe she simply was reacting the same way DJ had done.

"Or, if everyone thinks this is a bad idea," said Taylor in an aggravated tone. "I could just go downstairs and get drunk!" She stood and picked up her bag.

"No!" Eva stood. "Stop, Taylor!"

"Because it sounds a lot easier to me." Taylor was twisting the strap of her bag in her hands now. "And maybe I'm not as messed up as some people think. Maybe I'm just fine. I mean I was functioning. I get good grades. I'm—"

"No!" declared DJ. "I saw you sick as a dog this morning, wrapped around the toilet, barfing your brains out. And it's not the first time. Taylor, you told me that you drink daily—morning, noon, and night!"

Eva looked stunned. "Really?"

"Tell your mother the truth, Taylor."

"It's true. What DJ said."

"Oh … my!" Eva grabbed hold of the armchair as if to support her from falling.

194

"And it sounds like this is the best time to get into rehab," pointed out DJ. "Before New Year's."

Eva nodded. "That's true. I know this for a fact because of Taylor's father."

"You're right," said Taylor. "You're both right. But I need a drink so bad right now that I can't even see straight. I'm leaving!"

"No!" insisted Eva.

Now DJ stood. She went over to stand by Taylor. "Don't go," she pleaded.

"I *need* a drink," seethed Taylor.

"Here's what we'll do," said Eva suddenly. "I'll order room service. And I'll order you a drink or two, but you have to stay here."

Taylor seemed to be considering this.

"I'll call my manager, and he can arrange for your travel tomorrow. I'll do whatever I need to do to get you into the rehab place."

"But can I, *please*, have something to drink?" Taylor looked pitiful, like a child begging for candy.

"Yes, if you stay."

"And," added DJ, "if you hand over your fake ID."

Taylor looked alarmed now.

"That's right," said Eva. "If you want a drink, you need to show me your ID."

Taylor quickly produced the card and reluctantly handed it to her mom. Then DJ talked her into putting on sweats while Eva ordered up food and drinks.

It was a long night, but by the time it was over, it seemed all was in place for Taylor to travel to LA the next day. Because flights were booked, Eva's manager had arranged for Eva's tour bus to take Taylor. Then Taylor begged for DJ to go with her and return to Las Vegas on the same bus. She said she couldn't do it alone. And DJ was actually eager to go. She wanted to make sure that the rehab place was legit and not some weird cult.

But when the wake-up call came at five a.m., DJ wasn't so sure. Getting Taylor up and ready to travel was no easy task. By six they were packed and loaded onto the bus, which was actually very nice. The bus was barely on the road when both girls tumbled into the king-size bed and slept for several more hours.

By midafternoon, the bus pulled through a set of locking gates in front of what looked like an old hotel, positioned pleasantly by the ocean.

"Not bad," said DJ as they went inside.

"I guess." Taylor's hands were really shaking now. DJ suspected that Taylor wanted to make a run for it. Well, there was nothing DJ could do if she did. And for all DJ knew, she might make a run for it before the day ended.

DJ handed over the paperwork that Eva had given her, then she hugged Taylor and told her she loved her. After that Taylor was escorted down a corridor and DJ exited the building. Without saying a word to the driver, DJ got back on the bus, and before it was even back through the gates, DJ was sobbing. She wasn't even sure why. Maybe she was just tired or emotionally drained. Or maybe she just really cared about Taylor. DJ went back to the bedroom in the rear of the bus and closed the door. She knew that all she could do now was pray. And so she did.

DJ knew she should be grateful. She knew that she'd just participated in something totally amazing. Seriously, who ever would've dreamed that Taylor Mitchell would willingly go into an inpatient treatment program for alcohol addiction?

This whole crazy Vegas ordeal had been nothing short of a real living, breathing miracle. It was probably a life-saving miracle, because it was obvious that Taylor had been out of control and on the fast track to self-destruct.

God *had* answered DJ's prayers. He had truly intervened. DJ knew she should be thankful. And, really, she was. But at the same time, she was sad. Already she missed Taylor. And she felt worried and somewhat responsible. Like, what if it didn't work? What if Taylor wanted out?

Once again, DJ knew that all she could do was to trust God with the whole thing. He knew what was best for her and Taylor. And so far, at least once DJ had put her trust into him, he hadn't disappointed her. In fact, he had downright amazed her with this latest, greatest miracle.

The only problem now was ... *What am I going to tell Grand-mother?* DJ had promised to take good care of Taylor, to keep her safe and to bring her back for their big New York debut. What was DJ going to say to Grandmother now? That she had lost Taylor in Las Vegas? That she had somehow misplaced her friend, her grandmother's favorite protégé?

DJ knew it was time to pray again. Really pray. It was true that Taylor had been lost, but she'd been lost long before Las Vegas. And perhaps when it was all said and done, Taylor would be found. DJ could only hope. And pray.

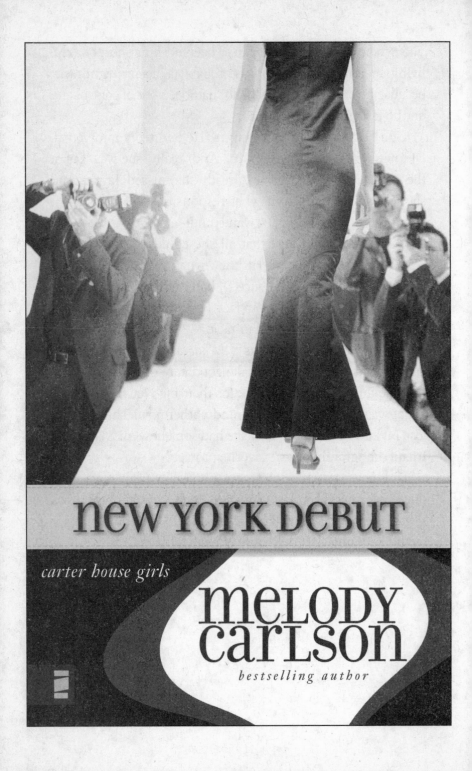

new york debut

carter house girls

melody carlson

bestselling author

Read chapter 1 of *New York Debut*,
Book 6 in Carter House Girls.

1

NEW YORK DEBUT

"**WHere Is Taylor?**" asked Grandmother as she drove DJ home from the airport. "Is she coming on a later flight?"

DJ hadn't told her the whole story yet. In fact, she hadn't said much of anything to Grandmother at all during the past week, except she left a message saying that she'd changed her flight and planned to be home two days earlier than expected. Obviously, Grandmother had assumed that Taylor had changed her plans as well.

"Taylor's in LA," DJ said slowly, wishing she could add something to that, something to deflect further questioning.

"Visiting her father?"

"No ..."

"Touring with Eva?"

"No ..."

"What then?" Grandmother's voice was getting irritated as she drove away from the terminal. "Where is the girl, Desiree? Speak up."

"She's in rehab."

"Rehab?" Grandmother turned to stare at DJ with widened eyes. "Whatever for?"

"For alcohol treatment."

Grandmother seemed to be stunned into speechlessness, which was a relief since DJ didn't really want to discuss this. She was still trying to grasp this whole strange phenomenon herself. It was hard to admit, but the past few days of being mostly by herself in Las Vegas had been lonely and depressing. She had really missed Taylor. The hardest part was when she discovered that Taylor wasn't allowed any communication from the outside. This concerned DJ. No cell phone calls, email, or anything. It seemed weird. And, although DJ was praying for her roommate, she was worried. What if it wasn't a reputable place? What if Taylor never came back? What if something bad had happened to her? Not only would DJ blame herself, she figured everyone else would too.

Finally Grandmother spoke. "Did you girls get into some kind of trouble out there in Las Vegas, Desiree?"

"No."

"I want you to be honest with me. Did something happen to precipitate this?"

"The only thing that happened is that Taylor came to grips with the fact that she has a serious drinking problem. If you'll remember, I tried to let you in on this some time ago."

"Yes, I remember the vodka bottle. I simply assumed it was a one-time occurrence."

"I told you otherwise."

"Well, I know that girls will be girls, Desiree. You can't have spent as much time as I in the fashion industry and not know this."

"Were you ever like that?" asked DJ. "I mean that 'girls will be girls' bit?"

Grandmother cleared her throat. "I wasn't an angel, Desiree, if that's what you're hinting at. However, I did understand the need for manners and decorum. I witnessed numerous young women spinning out of control. Beautiful or not, a model won't last long if she is unable to work."

"Isn't that true with everything?"

"Yes . . . I suppose. How long is Taylor going to be in . . . this rehabilitation place?"

"I don't know. You should probably call her mom."

"Oh, dear. That's something else I hadn't considered. Certainly Eva Perez won't be blaming me for her daughter's, well, her drinking problem."

"Eva is fully aware that Taylor had this drinking problem long before she came to Carter House."

"Good." Grandmother sighed and shook her head. "I just hope her treatment won't prevent her from participating in Fashion Week. That would be a disaster."

"Seems like it would be a worse disaster if Taylor didn't get the help she needs."

"Yes, of course, that goes without saying. But I would think that a week or two should be sufficient. Goodness, just how bad can a problem get when you're only seventeen?"

DJ shrugged, but didn't say anything. She thought it could get pretty bad, and in Taylor's case it *was* bad. And it could've gotten worse. To think that Taylor had been drinking daily and DJ never even knew it.

"It's just as well you came home early, Desiree," said Grandmother as she turned onto the parkway. "Already Casey and Rhiannon are back. And Kriti is supposed to return tomorrow. Eliza will be back on New Year's Eve."

"I'm surprised she didn't want to stay in France for New Year's."

"As am I. If I were over there, I'd certainly have booked a room in Paris. Nothing is more spectacular than fireworks over the City of Light. But apparently Eliza has plans with her boyfriend. Imagine—giving up Paris for your boyfriend!"

Of course, DJ knew that Eliza's life of lavish luxury didn't mean all that much to her. Like a poor little rich girl, Eliza wanted a slice of "normal." Well, normal with a few little extras like good shoes, designer bags, and her pretty white Porsche.

"It's good to be home," DJ proclaimed as her grandmother turned into the driveway.

"It's good to hear you say that," said Grandmother.

And it was the truth. After more than a week in Vegas, DJ was extremely thankful to be back. Maybe for the first time, Carter House did feel like home. And she couldn't wait to see Casey and Rhiannon.

"Welcome back," called Casey as she opened the door, dashed out onto the porch, and hugged DJ. "Need some help with those bags?"

"Thanks." DJ studied Casey for a moment, trying to figure out what had changed. "Your hair!"

Casey picked up one of DJ's bags, then grinned as she gave her strawberry blonde hair a shake. "Like it?"

"It's the old you—only better."

"My mom talked me into it. The black was a little dramatic, don't you think?"

"I think you look fantastic. And that choppy layered cut is very cute."

"Your grandmother approved of it too. And I got highlights."

DJ touched her own hair. "Taylor was nagging me to get mine redone. But it was so expensive in Vegas, I figured I'd do it here."

Casey lowered her voice. "So how'd your grandmother take the news about Taylor?"

DJ stopped at the foot of the stairs and stared at Casey. "Did Rhiannon tell you everything?"

"Yeah, is it supposed to be a big secret?" Casey made a hurt face now. "I was wondering why you told Rhiannon and not me. I thought we were friends, DJ."

"I didn't mean to, but I sort of spilled the beans with Rhiannon because I was so desperate and didn't know what to do at the time. But then I felt bad. I mean it was possible that Taylor wanted to keep it private, you know?"

Casey nodded somberly. "Yeah, I guess I do know."

"You should." After all, it had only been a few months since they had intervened with Casey in regard to her pain pill snitching.

"So, are you saying mum's the word?"

"Until Taylor comes back. Don't you think it's up to her to say something, or not?"

"Yeah. I can just imagine Eliza with that tasty little morsel of gossip. It'd be all over the school in no time."

"Speaking of Eliza, that means Kriti too."

"Kriti just got here about an hour ago." Casey paused, nodding toward the room that Kriti and Eliza shared. The taxi dropped her, and she went straight to her room. But something seems to be wrong."

"What do you mean?"

"I'm not sure. She just looks different. Kind of unhappy. I mean she didn't even say hello or anything."

"Maybe she was missing her family."

"That might be … but my guess is it's something more."

"We should probably try harder to reach out to her and make her feel at home."

"You're here!" Rhiannon burst out of the room and threw her arms around DJ. "Welcome home!"

"Man, it is so good to be back. Vegas—for more than a day or two—is a nightmare."

"At least you got a tan," observed Rhiannon. She glanced at Casey. "Both of you, in fact."

"It's that California sun."

"Don't make me envious," said Rhiannon.

"Hey, look at you," said DJ as she noticed that Rhiannon had on a very cool outfit. "Is that new?"

"Old and new. My great-aunt gave me some of her old clothes, and I've been altering them." She held out her hands and turned around to make the long circular skirt spin out. "Fun, huh?"

"And cool," said DJ.

"She's got all kinds of stuff," said Casey. "Hats and costume jewelry and scarves and things. I told her she should open a retro shop and get rich."

"Maybe I will someday."

"Or just sell things here in Carter House," suggested DJ. "Between Eliza and Taylor's clothing budget, you could clean up."

"Oh, yeah, DJ, Conner just called," said Rhiannon. "They just got back from their ski trip, and he said he tried your cell a few times, but it seemed to be turned off."

"More like dead. My flight was so early this morning, I forgot to charge it."

"Well, I told him you'd call."

Casey set DJ's bag inside her door. "Speaking of boys, I think I'll check and see how Garrison is doing—find out if he missed me or not." She touched her hair. "Do you think he'll like it?"

"How could he not," said Rhiannon. "It's so cool."

"Later," called Casey as she headed for her room.

"So, how's Taylor?" asked Rhiannon quietly.

"You didn't tell Kriti, did you?" whispered DJ, pulling Rhiannon into her room then closing the door.

"No, why would I?"

"I just wanted to be sure. I think we need to respect Taylor's privacy with this."

"Absolutely. So, have you talked to her?"

"They won't let me. They have this no-communication policy. No email, cell phones ... nothing. It's like a black hole. Weird."

Rhiannon nodded. "Yeah, it was like that with my mom at first. I think they wanted to keep her cut off from any bad connections. Then after a while, you earn communication privileges."

"Oh, that's a relief. I was really getting worried."

"I still can hardly believe Taylor went willingly."

"Yeah, our strong-willed, wild child ... putting herself into rehab." DJ shook her head.

"That reminds me, Seth has called a few times too. He wanted to know why Taylor's cell was off and where she was."

"What'd you say?"

"That I didn't know." She shrugged. "Actually, that was the truth."

"But nothing else?"

"No."

"Good. I mean, it's not like we need to keep it top secret, but until we hear from Taylor, let's not talk about it."

"Sure." Rhiannon put a hand on DJ's shoulder. "And don't worry about her, DJ. She'll be fine."

"I know." DJ nodded as she put her bags on her bed and started to unzip them. But as soon as Rhiannon left, DJ wasn't so sure. What if Taylor wasn't fine? What if something went wrong? And what if it was all DJ's fault?

A Sweet Seasons Novel
from Debbie Viguié!

They're fun! They're quirky! They're Sweet Seasons—unlike any other books you've ever read. You could call them alternative, God-honoring chick lit. Join Candy Thompson on a sweet, lighthearted, and honest romp through the friendships, romances, family, school, faith, and values that make a girl's life as full as it can be.

The Summer of Cotton Candy
Book One

Softcover • ISBN: 978-0-310-71558-0

The Fall of Candy Corn
Book Two

Softcover • ISBN: 978-0-310-71559-7

The Winter of Candy Canes
Book Three

Softcover • ISBN: 978-0-310-71752-2

The Spring of Candy Apples
Book Four

Softcover • ISBN: 978-0-310-71753-9

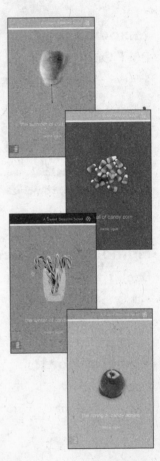

Book 4 coming soon!

Pick up a copy today at your favorite bookstore!

Visit www.zondervan.com/teen